J. Margot Critch current... ....
Newfoundland, with her h............................
two little buddies Simon a............. ....s equal
amounts of time writing, listening to Jimmy Buffett's
music and looking out at the ocean—all the while
trying to decide if she wants coffee or a margarita.

If you liked *Sins of the Flesh* why not try

My Royal Hook-Up by Riley Pine
Hard Deal by Stefanie London
Legal Passion by Lisa Childs

Discover more at millsandboon.co.uk

SINS OF THE FLESH

J. MARGOT CRITCH

MILLS & BOON

First Published in Great Britain 2018
by Mills & Boon, an imprint of HarperCollins*Publishers*
1 London Bridge Street, London, SE1 9GF

© 2018 Juanita Margot Critch

ISBN: 978-0-263-93233-1

MIX
Paper from
responsible sources
FSC™ C007454

This book is produced from independently certified FSC™ paper
to ensure responsible forest management.
For more information visit www.harpercollins.co.uk/green.

Printed and bound in Spain
by CPI, Barcelona

For Michelle. You've been a constant source of knowledge and support, and I'm so proud to call you my mentor and friend.

This one is for every woman reading this who has ever been told to sit down, relax, be quiet, let the men handle it. It's for every woman breaking down walls, smashing glass ceilings, fighting for her rights in an unfair system.

We've come a long way, baby. But we aren't done yet.

Resist, persist, exist.

We'll change the world.

CHAPTER ONE

"WHEN YOU LOOK at a man like Rafael Martinez, you can see he's really got it all. Being male, rich, influential. He knows the right people, and he knows how to strike a deal," Jessica Morgan said on television, as if she was looking through the camera, directly at Rafael as she spoke his name. "But the people of Las Vegas need, deserve, a mayor who is attuned to the needs of their community. Someone who understands the housing and welfare issues we face. I do. I'm running for mayor to help the people, the women and children who need someone to protect them and their rights. I want a more accountable, community-focused city council—"

Rafael bit back a curse and hit Mute on the remote control. So, he could still see the beautiful woman on the large flat screen in his living room, but not hear her slanderous words.

"Well, she isn't exactly wrong," Alex Fischer, his best friend said, smiling, from the couch. "You are male, rich and influential, and you know how to strike a deal."

Rafael glared at him, but didn't respond.

Alex relented, and leaned back casually. "Okay, so where did she even come from? And why does she have it out for you?"

"Jessica's been a city councillor for two years, since the last election, and she's been involved in community issues from the start. But with a few exceptions when we haven't seen eye to eye on certain issues, she's always been fairly quiet, and no one expected her to announce her candidacy." Rafael had thought her intention to run was a joke at first. He thought he'd be the hands-down successor to Mayor Thompson, and he had been just as surprised as everyone else when she'd become his opposition.

"So, she just up and decides to run for mayor?" Alex asked skeptically. "There has to be more to the process than that."

Rafael shook his head. "She only has to submit an application, have the money, campaign her ass off and hope to win. And guessing by the amount of press she's been getting, she is definitely doing that. And get this— she actually crowdfunded the money for her campaign. And raised lots."

"Are you kidding? And what's her problem with you? She clearly isn't a fan."

"No, she is not." His entire life, it didn't matter to him whether or not he was well liked. He was confident, secure enough to let the opinions of others, good and bad, roll off his back. He needed a thick skin to survive in politics. But he didn't know why Jessica Morgan's negative opinion of him dug at him. They'd had some friendly enough interactions in the past. But now the stakes had never been higher for him. The woman who was bad-mouthing him was his only opposition for the job he wanted, the job that was rightfully his.

"You got me. All I can think is that she wants to win. I'm the only other candidate, the one she has to beat," he said bitterly, recalling the slight dip in his approval rating since Jessica's entrance in the campaign. "She's got her fighting gloves on."

"So, what are you going to do about her? She can do a lot of damage to your campaign, talking about you like that. The last thing you need is to be portrayed as just another rich, elite asshole," Alex, who was also his campaign manager, needlessly reminded him.

"You think I don't fucking know that?" Rafael said, looking toward the screen at Jessica as she still spoke, now muted.

But Rafael wasn't just another *rich, elite asshole*. Hell, everything that Rafael had ever achieved, he'd worked his ass off for it. Every luxury he'd been afforded—the opulent home, the fast cars—were a direct result of the blood, sweat and tears that he poured into everything he undertook. Ever since he was a kid, his parents, Mexican immigrants who'd come to America for a better life, had instilled in him the knowledge that hard work begot success. And it was that belief that fueled his ambition in his business ventures and drove his political bid to be mayor of Las Vegas.

But he wasn't going to stop there. With his best friends and business partners—The Brotherhood, as they called themselves—at his back, he'd be unstoppable. Alex and their other friend Brett were local real estate moguls who ran one of the city's biggest firms. Gabe was one of the city's prominent lawyers and the group's legal expert. Alana, The Brotherhood's only female member, was a talented interior designer who also managed the group's various clubs and restaurants. Political influence was Rafael's contribution to the group. Together, they owned some of the most lucrative businesses in the city, and they were constantly looking to expand.

He turned away from Alex and gazed out the glass door to his backyard, looking past the hot tub and the pool, out at the darkened sky of Las Vegas, where the lights of the Strip and downtown beckoned to him. But if he looked beyond the lights, the glitz, the glamor, that Las Vegas was known for, he could see the rest of the city, full of the people he wanted to help. The people who, like his parents, had built homes and lives in the inhospitable, scorching desert, and sometimes struggled, working toward the American dream. Despite what Jessica Morgan *thought* she knew about him, he wanted to be the mayor of the people. He had the ideas, he had the connections, he had the money, and it wasn't just his ego driving him. Rafael just wanted to make a difference in the world. And for him, business growth that benefitted everyone in the local economy was a key way to do that.

But his career path went much further than that. He not only wanted to help elevate the people of Las Vegas, but deep down, he really wanted to help the people of the state of Nevada, and then America as a whole. He looked around his home, and while it was lavish and contained every comfort he could ever imagine, it wasn't enough; the money wasn't enough for him anymore. He'd set his sights high, and since he was a child, he'd dreamed of someday sitting in the Oval Office, being the commander-in-chief, leading the country, making decisions for the betterment of everyone in America, no matter who they were, working with other world leaders to make the world a better, safer, cleaner place. It would be tough, a lot of hard work, but Rafael was ready. He'd been preparing all his life for the battle and would take it head-on. There was only one thing standing in his way at that moment—Jessica Morgan.

He turned around, and his eyes narrowed as they zeroed in on the television once more, on Jessica Morgan's heart-shaped face, her green eyes, pouty lips. Her smooth, creamy skin that his fingertips itched to caress, and her light brown wavy hair, which was lightened throughout and at the ends with honey-colored highlights. Her message was one of equality, of everyone having a place at the table, and while he admired that message, he'd yet to hear her plan of how to accomplish it. As far as he was concerned, as idealistic as her message was, she was all talk.

But not only was she a bleeding heart, Jessica was a beautiful woman. Rafael couldn't deny that. She dressed conservatively, but the suits and high-collared shirts actually put more of her delicious curves on display than they hid, and that could easily drive a man to distraction. There were more times than he'd care to admit in the past two years, sitting across from her at council meetings, when he'd found himself preoccupied, wondering what she must look like under all the layers of clothing, or how her light brown hair would feel tangled around his fingers as his mouth took hers. He'd been called out several times already, not paying attention at public events because he was thinking about her pink lips wrapped around his cock...

"She's good-looking." Alex's observation broke through his thoughts, and he turned around to face his friend.

Rafael nodded, but didn't respond. It wasn't just her looks or raw sex appeal, Jessica had already proven herself to be strong, intelligent, passionate and one hell of a competitor. If the first few weeks of her campaign was any indication, he was in for a fight. It was imperative that he forget how good the woman looked and renew his focus on winning. He turned back to Alex, and saw his friend watching him.

"And that obviously didn't escape you," Alex noted. "Did Harris find out anything about her?" he asked, referring to the private investigator Rafael had hired to help him gain an edge in the mayoral race.

"I'm expecting him over here any minute now," Rafael told him. "He's been on her since the day she entered the race. That's why I called you over tonight. Apparently, he's got a bombshell to drop, and as my campaign manager and closest brother, I wanted you here for it." Alex might not have been his brother by blood, but since they were children, they'd been inseparable. All the members of The Brotherhood were close, but he and Alex shared a special bond.

Alex walked over to the wet bar and, helping himself to some of Rafael's good stuff, poured himself a couple of fingers of bourbon. "Sounds juicy. Want a drink?"

Rafael refused. "No, I need to stay sharp for tomorrow. I've got a luncheon with little old church ladies, probably shouldn't go in reeking of booze."

With a shrug, Alex sipped. "You don't know how some of those little old church ladies like to party." He snickered. "But you have fun with that. You have no idea what Harris wants to talk about?"

"No. He wouldn't tell me what it was until he was 100 percent certain, and he didn't want to do it over the phone." He grimaced at being told to wait. Rafael wasn't exactly the patient sort. "But I'm definitely intrigued. It sounds like he's got something big."

As if on cue, the doorbell chimed. Rafael smiled and walked out of the room to the door. He opened it, and Harris, his trusted PI, stood on the other side. He moved aside and let the man in.

"Tell me you've got something good," he said, as the two of them joined Alex in the living room.

Harris smiled. "Tell me if this is good," he said, as he passed over a brown envelope. Not wasting any time, Rafael opened it. His eyes widened with what he saw in the enlarged photos; the lighting might have been low in them, but they were of excellent quality. "I'll email these to you, too."

He turned to Harris. "Are these legit? Is it her?"

"I saw her with my very own eyes," the PI confirmed. "Last weekend in San Francisco, she was there, live and in person."

"What do you have there?" Alex asked, coming up behind him.

He passed over the photos to Alex, and smiled. "I think I just won this election."

Jessica Morgan leaned back in her chair. Now that the camera was off, she was finally able to relax. Despite the late hour, the live interview had gone well, and she hoped that it would help to raise her approval rating against Rafael Martinez. Jessica had come home exhausted after a long workday and still needed to pack for San Francisco; but when Tanya Roberts, the LVTV political reporter, had called requesting an interview to fill some time in their nightly broadcast, Jessica had no choice but to agree. She didn't have the resources her competitor did; she didn't have a ton of money to pour into television ads or flashy billboards. Along with her social media presence, and arranging informal meet and greets, she had to take advantage of any opportunity available to get her message out there.

"Thank you, Jessica," Tanya said, leaning forward and shaking her hand.

"Anytime, thank you for making time for me." Jessica took a swallow from her nearby water bottle. Her nerves were slowly waning. She was more comfortable with some types of performances than others. Public speaking was never her forte, but since she'd taken her place on city council, she was getting better. "I was pretty excited when Gordon came to me with the message from your office. I'll take any free publicity I can get." Her campaign manager had been ecstatic.

"Speaking of, how is the crowdfunding going?"

"Excellent," Jessica told her. She'd started raising money just after announcing her candidacy. "The response has been better than I could have imagined. I certainly wouldn't be here if it wasn't for the people who have contributed, volunteered. This is a group effort, for sure."

"And how's the campaigning going?"

"Really well," Jessica told her. "I'm kind of exhausted all the time, there's a lot of work to be done, but I expected that. But it'll all be worth it once the ballots are counted."

"I'm sure it will. Good luck with the campaign."

"I really appreciate the support, thank you so much." Jessica stood, covertly checking her watch. It was almost 11:00 p.m., and even though she had a lot to do before bed, she was still glad she'd agreed to the interview.

Seeing Tanya and her cameraman to the door, Jessica said her goodbyes, and when she closed the door, she leaned against it, letting out a deep, tired sigh. She still felt a nervous excitement flicker through her system, the same one that always did the day before a performance. All that stood between her and a stage was packing her bag, getting a couple hours' sleep and a short flight to San Francisco. And then she'd finally be able to fully relax, after burning off all the energy and tension she'd been carrying around since her performance last week. She knew from experience that the only effective way to dispel the stress was to get on a stage… *or a hot guy*, she mused, letting her thoughts flitter and linger on her opponent, Rafael Martinez, and his dark, supermodel good looks.

She shook her head; neither was an option at the moment. Certainly not within the city limits of Las Vegas, and definitely not while she was campaigning to be its mayor.

And certainly never with Rafael Martinez.

When she won, she knew she'd have to say goodbye to the stage. She would be under the microscope, and there was no way she'd be able to keep her other career a secret. So, as much as it pained her, and no matter how much she loved dancing, she had to stop.

Despite her ambitions, the prospect of a new life left her frustrated and tense. With no way to dance or have sex, to have a physical release tonight, a glass, *or a bottle*, of wine and her trusty vibrator would have to do. Jessica walked to the kitchen and dug out a bottle of wine from the cupboard. She poured a glass and brought it to the living room, then flopped down on the couch, turning on the TV to the news program that had just aired her live interview. But the first thing she saw was Rafael Martinez's face. Frustrated, she groaned. She just couldn't escape him.

Rafael was tall, dark and handsome, sexy, muscular, smart—just how she liked her men. It was a fact she'd tried to ignore in the past, but it was harder now in the throes of the campaign, seeing his face, hearing his name, at every turn. But she couldn't entertain thoughts of being attracted to the man. He was the enemy. He stood for everything she was against, and she needed to get him out of her head in order to concentrate on the job in front of her.

Despite herself, Jessica grabbed the remote, and instead of turning the TV off, she increased the volume. Even so, she could barely hear his words through the lust that clouded her senses. Essentially, she knew what he was saying, the same things politicians always talked about—*growth, industry, lowering crime yada yada yada*, the things that would gain him favor with his friends in the business community. Rafael talked a good game, though, she had to admit. He was smart, passionate, smug…gorgeous, drop-dead sexy, with his muscles that bulged and tensed through his dress shirts, his dark eyes that bore into those of whoever he was talking to, the full lips that parted to reveal straight, white teeth. His firm jawline, his nose straight, cheekbones high. It all combined to make him one irresistible man. *If only he wasn't so egotistical, stubborn, condescending, sexy…*

The front door opened and closed, the noise startling her, forcing her to jerk back from the television. Fumbling for the remote to turn off the TV, she dropped it, but in the process, she'd paused it.

"Girl, you will not believe the date I just had," her roommate and best friend, Ben, told her as he walked into the living room. He stopped and looked at Jessica, taking in her flushed complexion and jagged breaths. Cocking his head to the side, he laughed. "What are you doing? You look like I just caught you in the middle of a little *downstairs DJ*." He moved his fingers in small circles, mimicking the movements of working a turntable, but making a not-so-innocent implication.

Jessica tossed a throw pillow at him and leaned back on the couch. "Oh, shut up," she muttered, before she laughed. "Okay, what happened on your date? Was he cute?" She hoped to change the topic.

"He was extremely cute, a fireman, but dumb as a post. He thought that *alfresco* was the name of the guy who owned the restaurant," he answered, grabbing her glass from the coffee table and taking a sip of her wine. Then he nodded at the television, where the picture of Rafael, his perfect white smile, and those deep dimples, were frozen on the screen. "But, baby girl, I want to know what's got you looking so flushed here alone on the couch. Is it Mr. Martinez? He is certainly tasty."

"No," she said too quickly. "It's not him. You know, Ben, I'm not like you, I can control myself even around the most marginally good-looking guy." She stood.

Ben gestured to the TV. "Marginally good-looking? Look at this guy. I just wish he played for my team."

"Well, maybe you should sleep with him, then. But I'm going to bed. I've got to pack, I have to be on an early flight to San Francisco tomorrow morning."

"Aww, you're heading there again?"

"Yeah. Why?"

"I get so lonely on the weekends when you're gone. Why go to San Fran every weekend? There are strip clubs in Vegas, you know. That way I wouldn't have to miss you all the time."

"You know I can't risk dancing here. I can see the headlines now, Las Vegas City Councillor and Mayoral Hopeful Bares All Onstage!" She took her glass back from Ben. "And with the way the media have been following Rafael and me around, it would definitely get out."

"But what about when you get closer to the election? I assume you'll be hanging up the clear heels and the G-string for the glamour of the mayor's sash, or are you going to be America's first mayor-slash-exotic dancer?"

She laughed. "You know I don't own any clear heels. I'm not embarrassed of my career. I love absolutely every moment onstage. I'll miss it when it's over. But you know this city as well as I do." To tourists, Las Vegas could be considered more of a risqué city, but she knew that outside the famed Strip, the desert city more or less leaned conservative, and voters would not approve of her side job. She knew it was a risk to dance even now, but going out of state helped, and the money she earned helped with her campaign expenses. "So, it's time to leave it all behind. I knew that I couldn't dance forever. And there are things I need to do. It's time to focus my attention on helping people, and making the city better. I've got to be the change I want to see in the world."

"Trade the pole for a podium."

"Exactly. I'll miss the money, though," she said. But that wasn't it. Early on, stripping had been a way for her to make money and pay for college. But eventually, she realized she had a great flair for it. After a lot of hard work, she became well-known around the country for her skills with the pole. Being onstage was an empowering, fun, great exercise and she was extremely good at it, and high in demand. "You want to come with?"

"Nah, I've got another date with Mr. Cute-but-Dumb-as-a-Post. I just might invite him over, take advantage of having an empty house."

"Remember the pants-on-in-the-kitchen rule," she reminded him.

"That's your rule, not mine. But seriously, though, what's your plan for how you're going to beat him?"

"I'm going to beat him by being the best candidate."

Her roommate looked at her skeptically. "Is that going to be good enough? Why don't you let me talk to some people…see if we can dig up a little dirt on him."

"What *people* do you know?"

"I know people who know people."

She shook her head. "I don't think so. I don't want to win with underhanded tricks."

"You think Rafael Martinez doesn't know any underhanded tricks? I'm just saying that maybe you'll find out something interesting about him."

"I don't know," Jessica said, leaning in to give her

friend a kiss on the cheek. "Sounds sketchy. I've really got to get ready now, though. I'll see you on Sunday."

"Bye, baby girl, have fun in San Francisco."

"I intend to."

CHAPTER TWO

THE NEXT NIGHT, Rafael walked into Charlie's Gentleman's Club, which he'd learned was one of the classier strip clubs in San Francisco. The space was dark, like many nightclubs, and most of the light came from the stage, which was highlighted in yellow-and-red up-lights. A woman was on the stage, naked but for a G-string and a pair of platform heels, dancing to a classic rock song, and he watched her with some interest. He might have enjoyed the show more if he hadn't been there strictly on business. The woman, though gorgeous and talented, wasn't the woman he was there to see.

He stopped at the bar and ordered a beer, and turned around on the barstool to watch the stage. Charlie's was not anywhere near as seedy as he'd imagined it would be. It was clean, hip and filled with mixed patrons who were all respectful and well behaved, as they took in a show and socialized.

From being in the nightclub business himself with Di Terrestres, The Brotherhood's erotic members-only club, he knew that a safe and clean environment was the most important factor. Their club was a popular Las Vegas gathering place, an erotic playground for its exclusive clientele on every night of the week. They were the only thing like it in the city, and he was glad that he and his friends had clinched the market early on. Di Terrestres was the crown jewel of all their combined ventures and had proven to be their most profitable. In fact, being at Charlie's in San Francisco felt kind of like being at Di Terrestres in Vegas, except that here, Rafael most certainly did not have the home court advantage. This was Jessica's turf. But luckily, he had the element of surprise in his favor.

"Is Jessie M working tonight?" he asked the bartender over his shoulder.

She didn't respond at first, probably not too eager to talk to a random man who was looking for one of the dancers, in particular. She rolled her eyes and went back to her work, serving other thirsty patrons. Rafael slid a fifty across the bar top.

"Is Jessie working?"

The bartender looked at it before picking it up and slipping it under the low neckline of her tank top, which was almost bursting at the seams with ample breasts. "She's on in five minutes," she answered.

"Sounds like I'm just in time, then," he noted, and sipped his beer.

When the music quieted, Rafael turned back to the stage to watch the previous dancer leave, gathering her bills and clothing as she went. The buttery-voiced DJ came over the loudspeaker. "Everybody give Lola another big hand." After a burst of clapping from the audience, he played some prelude music as he spoke over the beat. "And now, ladies and gentlemen, we have a special treat for you. We don't see this lady perform here every day, but we love it every time she comes home. Tonight it is our pleasure to welcome, for one night only, the wonderful, sexy, award-winning, world-champion pole dancer, Jessie M, to our stage."

World champion? He turned at the sound of the huge round of applause, toward the stage in time to see a Las Vegas councilwoman, his main political opponent, the opinionated thorn in his side, Jessica Morgan, *Jessie M,* take the stage as her music, with its fast, steady, driving hip-hop beat filled the club.

She was confident and graceful, her movements quick, trained, controlled, completely in time with the music. She was passionate as she moved about the edge of the stage, making eye contact with every patron in the first couple of rows. He knew the look. It was the same she gave when she spoke one-on-one with a person. Sure, her gaze was somehow just as intent, but it was more intimate from the stage than it was when she spoke to her constituents or colleagues. He knew the passion was there no matter what job she undertook. And to Rafael, that was admirable. She gyrated on the stage and removed the top of her stage costume, revealing a rhinestone-covered bra that pushed her already high and full breasts to an unbelievable level.

When she approached the pole in the middle of the stage, Rafael pushed away from the bar and walked closer; then he took a seat at an empty table next to the stage. He almost missed it when, in one quick spin, she was at the top of the pole. She wrapped her legs around it and inverted her body, holding herself aloft with just the strength of her thigh muscles, gripping the metal, while somehow managing to still spin. With careful, deliberate moves, she lowered herself down the pole. He bit back a groan, as she spun again and held herself by her arms as she performed moves of acrobatics and flexibility, as if it were as natural as breathing. Rafael was in great shape himself, but he wasn't sure if he possessed the sheer strength that Jessica was exhibiting onstage while she worked the pole.

As he watched her, he felt his temperature rise as a flush of desire broke out all over his body. She might be his political rival. He might have gone to San Francisco to bust her. But goddamn, watching her perform was the hottest thing he'd ever seen. She stood in front of the pole and dipped low, spreading her legs. Then pushing herself back up and popping her round, firm ass at the audience, she undid the snap between her breasts with a quick flick of her fingers and shrugged off her bra.

Rafael's breath stopped in his chest as the article of lingerie hit the floor, the rhinestones clattering on the stage. Now topless, she held the pole and ground against it, her hips moving to the thrum of the music. She reached back and undid the bow that held her skirt together, and it fluttered to the floor, as well. Now wearing only a thong and her high-heeled shoes, she did a few more spins around the pole. Meanwhile, Rafael left his beer untouched, the rest of the room was forgotten, and he watched her as she swayed and swiveled under the spotlight, so comfortable there.

It was impressive, and Rafael sat back as Jessica commanded the crowd. She dropped to her knees on the stage, she crawled slowly over to him. Then, in a controlled movement that involved every muscle of her upper body, she pushed her chest down to the floor, and then arched her back, gracefully pushing herself up. Maintaining eye contact, as she danced for only him at the edge of the stage, Rafael reached into his wallet and pulled out a one-hundred-dollar bill. He stood close enough to slip the bill in the string of her thong over her hip, letting his fingers graze her soft skin. She winked at him and blew a sultry kiss, but the realization dawned in her eyes, followed briefly by panic, then fear. She knew it was him, but somehow schooled her reaction to keep cool, then she sauntered away as the lights dimmed and the music stopped. The crowd erupted in applause for Jessica. But Rafael took a seat, certain that she would come find him.

He sat stunned, his heart pounding, his dick straining against his zipper, as he watched his competitor in the Las Vegas mayoral race, almost naked, gathering her clothing and the various bills that had been thrown across the stage, trying not to look directly at him. He had shaken her. He'd gone to San Francisco to bust her, to make her quit her campaign, which would hand him a tidy victory by default. But something had sparked a change in him. He was no longer quite as interested in outing her, and now he was intrigued, and he wanted to know more about her. More than what she looked like dancing in a thong and high heels, he reasoned.

Oh, my God. Oh, my God. Oh, my God.

It was him.

Jessica stepped behind the curtain and emerged backstage, where the other dancers were preparing, chatting, lounging between their own performances. She'd danced a great set, and performing always left her with a rush and gloriously fatigued muscles. She relished the lights, the applause, but she'd almost passed out when she saw Rafael Martinez standing next to the stage. The bill he'd slipped into her G-string was still there, wedged between the polyester and her hip. She could still feel the way his fingers had grazed her skin as she pulled it out, frowning when she saw the denomination. A hundred dollars? *What is he doing here?*

She'd been able to keep her cool out on the stage, when she'd looked down and realized it was him sitting there, front row. Rafael Martinez. He was in her club, he'd seen her dance and now everything was over for her. He was there to bust her, he would tell everyone that she was a dancer, ruin her career, her life, everything she'd worked for. So, she'd maintained eye contact with him when she recognized him, then she'd stood straight and held her head high as she left the stage.

The more she thought about it now, however, her bravado waned. Her hands shook, and she could barely maintain her grip as she fisted her costume, and her money. She had to get dressed and face him. Reminding herself that she had nothing to be embarrassed about, she felt her anxiety diminish. But she knew that in his hands, he held the power to destroy her dreams. She had to see what he was doing there, and somehow try to convince him to keep her secret.

"Hey, great set, Jessie," one of the other girls said, but she couldn't be sure who said it. She was too focused on figuring out a way to save everything she stood to lose. She dressed quickly in a skirt and T-shirt, and toyed briefly with cutting out the back door, to get away without seeing Rafael, or even siccing one of the bodyguards on him. But neither of those things would solve her problem. She would have to see him at some point, better here at her regular club than at a debate. Taking a deep breath, Jessica steeled her resolve and stepped out from the back room to find him.

She looked around the club and, ignoring the glances of the patrons who'd just seen her perform, she found Rafael almost immediately, sitting at the table near the stage, casually sipping from his beer bottle and already watching her, his lips curved upward in a smug, amused smirk. *Goddamn him.* Straightening her shoulders, portraying what she hoped was an air of confidence, she walked toward him.

Taking a seat, she slid his one-hundred-dollar bill across the table to him, then leaned back. "I'm not taking your money," she told him, crossing her arms.

"Then how will I pay for my private dance?" Rafael asked, his right eyebrow raised. "I'm a customer."

The man was unbelievable. "You aren't getting one. And I don't care who you are. I don't do private dances. I haven't in years."

"This is a good time to break that streak, isn't it?" he asked with a sly smile.

"If I did, you certainly wouldn't be the recipient. What are you doing here?"

"I could ask you the same thing," he returned, taking an easy look around the club. She followed his eyes, watching women casually stroll through, wearing skimpy lingerie, if they were dressed at all.

She scowled. A new dancer had come out and the attention of everyone else in the club had turned to the stage as music filled the room. "Are you going to answer any of my questions?"

He shrugged. "I don't think I need to. I'm the one who's here for answers."

She sighed. "What do you want?"

He lifted his wrist, and she saw from the large face of his Hublot watch that it was after 3:00 a.m. She rolled her eyes at him—that watch could pay her mortgage for at least a couple of months. Such pointless luxury. Yeah, he was certainly a man of the people, she thought with scorn.

"What do I want?" he repeated. "Well, right now, I kind of want an early breakfast," he told her, leaning across the table. "Want to join me?"

She looked at him, in his casual clothing. He looked good in his suits, but in street clothes, he looked great. *No*, she didn't want to go anywhere with him, and she was about to tell him as much, but she needed to figure out what his plan was with his new information. It had been a while since she'd eaten, and betraying her, her stomach rumbled loudly. "There's a twenty-four-hour diner a couple doors down if that suits you. They have a pretty good breakfast menu. Unless you want something fancier, but in this neighborhood, you might be out of luck. And—" she gestured to his watch "—you probably shouldn't flash that piece around here."

"I'm not too worried about it. I can defend myself if I need to. But that diner sounds great," he said with a smile, standing. "Let's go."

Being seated across from Rafael in the diner was a surreal experience for Jessica. She was physically tired from her performance, but she was mentally exhausted trying to figure out a way out of her current predicament, afraid that her secret would ruin her, but she couldn't help looking at Rafael, regarding him quietly, trying to figure him out.

She had always been attracted to him, since the day she'd first met him. But she'd never let herself get close to him, and on only a few occasions had she ever been one-on-one with him. The reason why? Those dark brown eyes, his deep, low voice that flowed from his lips, effortlessly transitioning between Spanish and English. He was normally so polished, looked every part the well-put-together politician. But at three o'clock in the morning, the dark shadow of a beard colored his strong jaw and his hair was slightly disheveled, and it made her fingers itch with the need to reach across the table and smooth it. He looked rugged in nice but worn jeans and a fitted black V-neck T-shirt. It showed that there might be more to him than the arrogant politician-slash-businessman.

They looked at each other, not saying anything. She imagined that, like her, he was trying to figure out what to make of their current situation. Silent, until the shadow of the waitress fell over their table.

"What can I get for you folks?" she asked them, barely looking up at them from her notepad, seemingly unaware of the tension that radiated between Jessica and Rafael.

"I'll have a coffee," Rafael said.

"How do you take that?"

"Black."

"And you, hun?" She turned to Jessica.

"I'll have tea. Something herbal, if you got it."

"Lemon okay?"

"Sounds good."

"Any food?"

"No." She shot a pointed look at Rafael. "I'm not hungry." She was, in fact, starving, but she couldn't afford to spend any longer in his company than she needed to.

The server turned to Rafael, pen poised to take his order. "Nothing else for me, either. Thanks."

When the waitress walked away, Jessica folded her arms and leaned across the table. "I thought you wanted breakfast."

"Well, I don't want to order food if you aren't going to have any. I can't have you seeing my food, getting jealous and stealing any of my bacon." He said, serious, before flashing a bright smile at her.

Flabbergasted, Jessica shook her head. Rafael had her at his whim, and he sat there *joking*. "So, what now?" she asked him, ignoring his attempts at humor. She needed to get down to business. "Are you going tell the press? Or leak the fact that I strip online? Or just plain old blackmail me into dropping out of the mayoral race altogether?"

Rafael honestly seemed to consider his response. "That was my first thought. But, you know, it's not really my style to go to the press. Maybe I've had a change of heart. I'm not a snitch. And God knows I've got my share of skeletons."

"Oh, really? So, what then? What are we doing here?"

He shrugged. "Intrigue, maybe? I guess I was curious why a fairly popular city councillor and mayoral candidate has stripping as a side gig."

"Only fairly popular? Check the latest polls, bud."

"Polls don't mean anything," he said with a wave. "Up, down, whatever. The only thing that matters is election night."

She sighed. "I'm going to ask once more—what are we doing here? It's late, and I'm too tired for this."

"Why do you do it? Is it the money? Councillors make a decent salary."

The waitress reappeared with her tea and Rafael's

coffee. When she shuffled off again, they both sipped from their cups until Jessica spoke again. "It's fun, it's empowering and I'm good at it. And it isn't a side gig. For a long time, stripping was my full-time job. I know I won't be able to do it for much longer without being found out, especially not when I'm mayor."

"You are good at it. One of the best I've seen." He nodded and looked her over. His heated gaze made her breath halt. "You're still so confident that you're going to win? I'm also curious what the more conservative Las Vegans would think about your job when they find out?"

She said nothing, bristling at the implication, still unsure of what his plans were. "*When* they find out? I thought you weren't going to tell."

He chuckled, and the sound resonated deep within her, and she realized that she'd never heard him laugh before. Hell, she'd barely even had a conversation with him. And damn him, she was starting to like it. He took a sip of coffee and leaned closer. "Why don't we get out of here?" he asked, his deep and dark tone told her exactly where he wanted to go with her.

She stilled. And that was it. Angry words bubbled to her mouth. She leaned across the table and pointed her finger in his face. "I'm not going to sleep with you to keep your mouth shut. You can forget that."

He blinked quickly, and paused, as if he were trying to choose the right words. "Trust me, sweetheart, I've never had to resort to blackmail to get a woman into my bed. I'm not about to start now." His eyes searched her upper body, and she felt the burn from them. "No matter how good of an idea it might be." She remained unconvinced, and tried to stop herself from thinking about him getting her into his bed. He kept going, and she had to focus her attention to hear what he was saying. "You clearly have the wrong idea about me," he started. "You don't seem to like me very much."

A shocked laugh made its way past her lips. "How fragile are you? Is that what you're worried about? People not liking you? So what if I don't? You're everything I don't like, everything that's standing in the way of real change."

"No, not quite." He held up his hand, cutting her off. "I know that there are quite a few people around town who don't like me, and I don't care. But for some reason, I'm just concerned about *you* not liking me." He paused to let it sink in. "I'm not a bad guy, Jessica, really. And even though you think you know a lot about my life and my upbringing, you really don't. And that's unfortunate. And seeing as how we're spending so much time together lately, going to the same events, I think we should get to know each other."

She rolled her eyes, used to having men propose that they *get to know each other*. "I'm sure you do."

"Come on." He smiled. "My closest friends, at least four people who aren't blood-related, agree that I'm actually a pretty great guy."

"And what if I already feel like I know enough about you?"

He yawned. "You know, it is pretty late. We should probably go. My flight leaves in a couple of hours."

"Wait. We aren't done discussing what you're going to do with the information you plan to hold over my head." His constant switching of gears, changing the conversation, had her experiencing whiplash.

He shrugged. "I don't know what I'm going to do with it yet. Maybe I'll give you the opportunity to plead your case. Spend some time with me when we get back to Vegas. I'm sure we can talk through this."

"I don't have time to spend with you. I have to work."

"Stripping or campaigning?"

She seethed. "Campaigning. I don't strip in Vegas."

"That's unfortunate for Vegas." He frowned, looking her up and down. She was grateful for the table, as it stopped his gaze from lighting the rest of her on fire.

Jessica looked across the table at him. His dark brown eyes were warm, disarming and held the slightest bit of humor. Part of her knew all she needed to know about Rafael Martinez—that he was a self-interested businessman. It wasn't common knowledge just how deeply lined his pockets were, or just how well connected he was in the local business scene, but she'd learned enough in her time working with him to know he wasn't what Las Vegas needed right now. But she was attracted to him, there was no denying that. Just looking at him stirred the interest between her thighs. Maybe the other part of her wanted to get to know him in a physical way. Either way, she was too exhausted to put up much of a fight. She wanted to sleep, and she would let her brain and her loins fight it out tomorrow. She blew out an impatient breath. "Fine. What do you have in mind?"

"I don't know. How about dinner tomorrow night? A drink or two. We'll talk."

"We can talk now."

He looked around the restaurant. "Nah," he told her, shaking his head. "Let's do it when we get back to Vegas."

"I get it. You want the hometown advantage, hey?"

He grinned again. "Maybe you know me better than I thought."

Her energy was flagging, and she knew she wouldn't be able to stand up to him much longer. "Okay, fine, I'll have dinner with you." She could spare at least an hour, to talk to him and keep her secret life exactly that. She paused. "This sounds an awful lot like blackmail, though." He was sipping his coffee, but his eyes smiled at her from behind the mug. "So, how did you find out I was here?"

"I don't know how that matters." He shrugged. "I found you, either way."

Unbelievable. His reluctance to tell her made her angry. "Are you not going to tell me anything? How dare you just waltz into my personal life and completely turn it upside down by holding this over my head, and then not even explain how you found out?" She watched him, noting how sure and confident he was, sitting in the booth. She rolled her eyes, put down her mug of tea and stood. She threw a twenty-dollar bill on the table for the tab—she didn't want to owe him anything. "I don't have time for your mind games, Rafael. I'm tired, and I just want to go back to my hotel."

He stood after her. "Jessica, wait. I'm not letting you leave alone in a neighborhood like this."

Feeling the rage rise from her core, she huffed out a breath. "You know, I feel safer in a *neighborhood like this*, than I do in *your world*," she sneered, then turned away from him and headed for the door. "Where a man can just steamroll over another person, with no warning, no reason. You know what? I'm done with you. Tell people whatever you'd like." She just wanted to get away from him.

"Jessica, wait," he called again, and she turned in time to see him also throw a twenty on the table. At least their waitress would have a good tip. He caught up to her. "At least let me get you a cab."

"I can get my own cab."

He looked up and down the street, and saw the road was empty but for a lone taxi coming toward them. It stopped, and Rafael opened the back door for her. "Mind if I share? There don't seem to be any others around."

Jessica thought about refusing, but she looked him over in his designer jeans and her gaze snagged on that watch. Pretty boy wouldn't last a second. No matter what she thought of him, any harm that befell him would be on her hands for leaving him there. "Whatever. Come on." She shuffled inside the cab, but she found herself against the hard plastic of a child's car seat that was strapped into place behind the driver, unable to move beyond the middle seat. Rafael then got in after her, firmly trapping her in her place.

Rafael was surprised by the lack of space in the back seat of the car, and the closed confines made him squeeze his body against hers so he could shut the door. His arm and thigh pressed against hers. Her skin was warm and smooth against his, and interest stirred deeply inside of him. The crackle of electricity that danced between them was like a live wire. He looked over at her, and she sat rod-straight, looking directly out the windshield, ignoring him entirely. He wondered briefly if she'd felt it, too. He shifted again, just to see, brushing her arm as he moved. He got his answer when she drew in a quick breath between her teeth, like a gasp, and she quickly shifted away from him, putting as much distance between them as she could. Which wasn't much.

"Where to?" the cabdriver asked. Rafael looked in the mirror and saw the eyes of the driver. Jessica gave him the address of her hotel.

"And you, buddy?"

"Drop the lady off first, then we'll worry about me," he said, not taking the chance that the driver would drop him off first. Rafael's protective nature pulled at him. This late at night, *well, early in the morning*, he wanted to make sure Jessica got to her hotel safely before he got out of the car. The driver shrugged, indifferent to Rafael's answer, and pulled away from the curb.

They drove in the tense silence of the car, their bodies pressed together. Every time Jessica tried to shift away from him, he felt her soft skin rub against his own, and the contact caused a familiar stirring in his groin. He'd always thought she was gorgeous, but Jesus, since seeing her performance on the stage, there was no fucking doubt that he wanted her. As his dick came to life in his lap, he tried to think of anything that would dissipate his desire. Baseball, *Antiques Roadshow*, Monopoly, the three-hour Easter vigils his mother dragged him to as a child. Nothing worked. He coughed to clear the lump in his throat.

Jessica was facing forward, looking out the windshield of the car as they made their way to her hotel. But Rafael kept his eyes on her. He'd harbored at least one or two (*dozen*) fantasies about the woman beside him, most of them capturing his imagination at the duller moments during their city council meetings, or during mind-numbing political dinners and fund-raisers. She was intelligent, tough, articulate, goddamn sexy. Since campaigning had begun, she always had an opinion about something he proposed, and she was a continual thorn in his fucking side. They were political opponents, and she took potshots at him any chance she got, while he did the same. But pressed against her in the back seat of a San Francisco taxi, all he wanted to do was kiss her. But he had to stop himself; he couldn't let on what he was feeling, and he hoped that the bulge of his stiffening dick wasn't plainly obvious to her. He looked down at her, her features highlighted in the light of the dash. She was beautiful, soft, vulnerable. As a man who was so normally in control of his desires, he tried to fight his need. But he wasn't sure he would win.

Perhaps feeling his eyes on her, Jessica turned her head and they locked eyes. The air between them was still charged. Jessica said nothing, but her lips parted; the movement was small, but he caught it. Before he knew he was doing, Rafael reached for her and, putting his palms on either side of her face, brought her lips to his.

She was hot, sweet, and the moment his lips hit hers, he knew she would either reciprocate, fall into his kiss, or smack him with rejection. At first, she was stiff, but when he took her bottom lip between his own, nibbling her lightly, she sighed and softened, yielding to him. She lifted her hands and fisted them in the front of his T-shirt as her lips parted with his. She tasted like lemon from the tea she'd had at the diner, and her tongue dueled with his as he tried to maintain control of the kiss.

He reached across her, unsnapped her seatbelt and pulled her into his lap, so that both of her legs draped over one of his thighs and his dick, rock hard, drove into her lush ass. The low ceiling of the car didn't give them a lot of room, and she had to duck her head. Her arms wrapped around his neck, her fingers fisting his hair, and he kissed her harder as she lowered them, running her hands over her shoulders, down his chest. Rafael was harder than he'd ever been in his life, and he needed to be inside of her.

He knew that they were in the back of a cab, and that they had an audience in the driver, but he didn't care, and from the way her lithe fingers made their way under his shirt, and up his chest, she didn't, either. The hand that rested on her bare thigh skimmed upward, until he was under her skirt. Her legs parted slightly, and he took it as an invitation to go further. When his fingers hit the satin barrier of her panties, he slipped past them and, again, she offered no resistance. He about shook with desire as his fingers found her hot flesh, already slick with her need. His fingers circled her clit, and she wrapped her arms around his shoulders, clutching him, pulling him closer. She cried into his mouth. Oblivious to the driver in the front seat, Rafael slid one finger and then another inside of her. She gripped his fingers from the inside, and he began to slide them in and out, as the heel of his hand pressed against her clit, his movement almost made effortless by how wet she was. He imagined that it was his dick, and he groaned into her mouth. Jessica's breathing quickened. Her every physical response, her shallow breath, the way she spread her legs wider, allowing him greater access, the small desperate sounds that she made in his mouth, told him that she was coming.

He considered taking her then and there, as his cock about threatened to burst through his jeans, and he would have, if not for the sound of a throat clearing from the front seat. The driver, requiring their attention. He pulled away from her long enough to look at the other man. *"Fuck,"* Rafael muttered.

"Miss, we're at your hotel," the driver announced, looking straight out the windshield.

"Oh, right," she said, her voice shaking, with her impending release, and his hand still between her legs, neither of them making any effort to move.

With one hand at the back of her head, he pulled her to him again, not letting her get away that quickly. He kissed her again. "Invite me up," he told her, just a breath of electric air was all that separated them, his lips skimming hers with every word.

She said nothing, as he held his breath, waiting for the okay to go up with her and continue the night. But as the haze of desire cleared from her eyes, a look of shock replacing it, she gave him a soft "no" and pushed herself from his lap. "I can't."

His need for her numbed the surprise he felt by her refusal. Most women didn't refuse him, especially after he made them feel the way he just had. But Jessica was different. She disengaged from him, taking her seat next to him. He immediately missed her heat, her slight weight against his dick. And they both remembered that because of the car seat that blocked the door nearest her, he had to get out to release her. "Move, please," she said, her breath still heavy and matching his own.

He could have remained seated, insist again that they spend the night together. But she was right, and he knew it. *They couldn't. They shouldn't.* So, he nodded and got out of the car, adjusting the near-painful erection that threatened the integrity of his jeans zipper. She stood and opened her purse and withdrew her wallet.

"I've got the taxi," he said. "Don't worry about it."

"I pay for my own ride," she told him, putting some

money on the back seat of the car, and before he could insist she take it back, she was already halfway to the hotel door. Rafael got back into the cab and blew out a breath. Jessica might pay for her own ride, but he knew that he would pay dearly for it, as well.

CHAPTER THREE

By Sunday evening, Rafael was beat. He'd flown back to Vegas from San Francisco early that morning, and he'd gotten right down to work. In addition to his work on the city council, he also quietly oversaw the finances of The Brotherhood's operations; while he was left out of the group's decision-making, he was still very much involved behind-the-scenes. While most conglomerates employed teams of people to oversee all facets of operations, The Brotherhood preferred to manage as much as they could by themselves. Some people could look at his business involvement and see a conflict of interest, if they knew how closely tied he still was to The Brotherhood. Rafael had never explicitly used his political power for the betterment of his friends, or his own business, but he'd always considered it using all of the tools at his disposal. It was just how things were done.

From his office in the BH, the commercial tower they'd erected that housed the headquarters of their respective companies, he was putting the finishing touches on his analysis of the previous quarter's profits. He closed his spreadsheets and turned his attention to a Word document he was working on. He heard his door open, and Alex walked in. The partners all had an open-door policy between them and rarely knocked before entering each other's offices. It was Sunday, but that didn't mean they weren't at work. There was a lot to do. A lot of balls to keep up in the air. Rafael raised his hand in greeting, and Alex took the seat on the other side of his desk. Rafael hadn't seen his friend since he'd returned.

"How was San Francisco?"

"Good," he said simply, not willing to provide any detail. Not looking up, he put the finishing touches on the report, trying to forget the way his body stiffened, remembering how he'd touched and kissed Jessica the night before.

Alex leaned forward in his chair. "So, what happened? Did you see her?"

"If you're so interested, maybe you should have come along."

"Dude, I told you. I had a date. That fortuitously turned into *two dates*," he said with a satisfied grin.

Rafael smiled, glad that Alex hadn't actually tagged along. "Well, good thing I gave you the weekend off from the campaign."

"But you need to tell me. Did you see Jessica? Was she at the strip club?"

Rafael didn't respond at first. He closed his laptop and looked at his friend. "I need you to keep what you know about her between us," he warned him.

"What? That doesn't make any sense."

"You can't tell anyone about what we found out about her, okay?"

Alex nodded. "Yeah, man. Of course. But why? This could hand you an easy victory. Why the change of heart?"

He ignored his friend's last question. He didn't even know the answer to that one. He had gone to California to bust her, to see firsthand the information that would win him the election. "I did see her," he confirmed, with a quick nod of his head. "And she was dancing. But I don't know what I want to do about it yet."

"What's to know? Just give us the okay to leak it to the press. Dude, this is what you want." He cocked his head to the side, eyes narrowing in understanding. "Did something happen between you and her?" he asked, suspicious.

"Nothing happened," Rafael responded. Except a kiss that completely scorched him to his core and left him with a burn no number of cold showers would heal. "But I decided that I don't want to win like that. I can win this election on my own. I don't need to ruin her in the process."

He could tell that Alex knew Rafael was hiding something. "What's going on?" his friend asked. "Just two days ago, you wanted to end her."

"Nothing's going on. Just give me a little time to wrap my head around this. Everything is fine. I assure you. Don't worry."

"Fine." Alex held up his hands in mock surrender.

"It's getting late. I was going to take off, but I stopped by to see if you wanted to head downstairs to the club and get a drink. See if there's anything fun going on."

The club, Di Terrestres, was their favorite business, their pet project, the crowned jewel of all The Brotherhood's operations. When they'd built the office building, they'd left the bottom floors empty for their own fun—a members-only adult playground for the elite. The sex club catered to almost any desire a consenting adult could have.

"Weren't you with two women last night?" Rafael asked, eyebrow raised at his friend's insatiable sexual appetite.

Alex shrugged and checked his watch. "That was like twenty-four hours ago."

Rafael thought of the beautiful women and everything else he could ever want waiting for him downstairs, and he sighed. None of it interested him at the moment. He needed sleep, and a certain petite, green-eyed brunette with a heart-shaped face, who occupied an office at city hall and the forefront of his fantasies. "No, I can't. I'm going home."

"Now I *know* something's going on."

"Dude, I haven't slept since Friday night. I'm allowed to take a night off from debauchery."

"Yeah, you're allowed, it's just never happened before." He stood. "All right, I'm done. I'm heading down. Join me if you want."

Rafael shook his head. Tired and horny, but with no way to ease either at Di Terrestres, he sat back. "I'll see you tomorrow."

CHAPTER FOUR

ON MONDAY MORNING, Jessica boosted the speed and incline on the treadmill and she ran, pumping her legs as a surge of energy coursed through her body. She couldn't get Rafael out of her head. He'd gone to San Francisco to what? Bust her, to show that he knew about her secret life?

She knew how to figure out men, they weren't complicated creatures, but Rafael was an enigma that she couldn't decipher. Waking up in her hotel room yesterday morning after only a couple hours of sleep, she'd felt hungover, as if she'd overindulged in alcohol, but she hadn't. So, she downed some coffee, and had then gone online, checking news sites and gossip rags. She'd even Googled her own name to see if he had leaked her secret life. And she'd found nothing. What was his game?

She thought about the night before, remembering that she hadn't been drinking, nothing but herbal tea. The only intoxicant she'd experienced had been the taste of Rafael's lips and the brush of his tongue. The stroke of his fingers.

And what about that kiss? And those hands... She ran harder, trying to rid herself of the memory of his lips and fingers on her. Her muscles screamed as the adrenaline flowed through her, and she remembered being trapped with him in the back of that cab. From the way he touched her, she knew he must be a spectacular lover. It was something she'd always suspected whenever she'd looked across the room to him at meetings, or when they met at functions. The way he held himself, the capable, confident swagger of a man in control. But with Rafael, it wasn't an act. Even keeping pace with the belt of the treadmill, she felt a desirous hollow between her thighs, one that she could fill with only him. Frustrated, she boosted the speed of the treadmill again, hoping to run it out.

But his knowledge made her vulnerable. He held her life, her career in the palm of his hand and could snatch it all away from her if the whim struck him. Everything she remembered from that night had actually happened, and it hadn't been her worst nightmare, or her hottest erotic dream. Not only did Rafael now know the secret that she'd successfully hidden for years as a city councillor, but she'd also about dry humped him in the back of a taxi. *What a goddamn mess.* She considered his proposition—spend time with him, get to know him, and maybe he wouldn't spill the beans. She didn't like the man, but to be fair, she didn't really know him. What she *did* know was that he had a hard, hot body and he kissed like a demon.

Her heart rate sped up, and it didn't have anything

to do with running. She looked up at the television and saw a newscaster was speaking with Rafael outside city hall. She took out her earbuds and turned the TV volume up to hear him over the sound of her feet pounding.

"I want to encourage business growth. And that's why we need to work with business owners in our city. All successful cities are built by the people first."

Jessica rolled her eyes. She hated his act of pretending to care about the little people, when it was clear he only cared about helping business owners. Since announcing his campaign, he'd been eager to talk about his upbringing in a middle-class, immigrant family. But no matter his background, he was now so far removed from anything middle class. He may have started out there, but what did he know about the struggle of the people now, while he looked down upon them from his ivory tower?

Jessica knew the people intimately. She'd devoted herself to community issues surrounding housing and social assistance since she'd become a councillor. Growing up, she'd made a point of volunteering regularly in her neighborhood—even now she would go across town once a month to help out at the shelter she'd become so familiar with as a young student. Looking back, it was probably no surprise she'd ended up in public office.

Rafael might have a good act, but she knew better.

But it didn't matter; he currently held the upper hand. He knew about her secret life. And even though he hadn't said anything yet, it didn't mean he wouldn't.

There were so few people that she trusted, and she was reluctant to add Rafael Martinez to that list.

Frustrated and fatigued, she pounded the end button on the treadmill's control panel. When the belt stopped, she hunched over the panel, breathing deeply. She knew better, but it didn't stop her from wanting the man more than she'd ever wanted anyone before.

Jumping down from the machine, Jessica took more calming breaths and drank her water. She picked up her phone and saw the text message from Ben telling her to call him. When she did, her friend sounded excited.

"Girl, have I got news for you."

"What is it?"

"It's about Dreamboat Martinez."

"What about him?"

"I found something out about him."

It was as if Ben had read her mind. "How did you know—"

"I've been talking to some people."

"Again with these mysterious people you know. I know for a fact you don't know people."

He laughed, but then turned serious. "Just listen to me. Have you ever heard of Di Terrestres?"

"Of course I have." Who hadn't. It was a well-known hangout for Las Vegas's superrich and the elite. But she'd never been inside. Not being rich, or elite, she'd never been invited through the front doors.

"What do you know about the *shadowy cabal* who runs it?" Ben asked. Jessica was running out of time and patience to play this guessing game.

"I've got stuff to do today, can you just save us some time and tell me?"

"I have it on good authority that Rafael Martinez is a silent partner of The Brotherhood, the extremely well-connected group that owns it and many other enterprises."

"Really?"

"Yeah, I heard a rumor and I got a friend of mine to do a little digging. It was tricky, but apparently Mr. Cute-but-Dumb-as-a-Post has some friends in high places. But this is some real information for you. What would staunchly conservative Las Vegans think of their golden boy owning a sex club within city limits?"

Jessica felt a smile grow on her lips. She finally had some leverage on the man who knew a truth about her. "Thanks, Ben. I know I told you not to dig, but I'm glad for once that you didn't listen to me."

"No problem, doll. Will you be home for dinner?"

"No," she said, her lips pursing as an idea formed in her head. "I've got plans tonight."

"It sounds like you've got something on your mind, and I want you to fill me in later."

"I will. Don't worry." Jessica hung up the phone, checked the time and realized that her workout had run long. She had a meeting with her team, and then she had an appearance to make at the university. Time to get her ass in gear and out the door.

Jessica took the time to talk to every student who'd shown up to meet the mayoral candidates and other members of council. It was part of a city initiative, in conjunction with the student union, to get young people interested in municipal politics. And judging by the crowd that had packed the student union building, people were interested. This high a youth turnout was almost unprecedented. The plan had worked, and it gave Jessica hope for the future generation and political engagement. Even the local TV news crews had shown up. She couldn't remember an election that had gotten so much coverage. People were fascinated by her, Rafael and the entire electoral process, and voter registration was high.

She looked across the room and saw Rafael and some of his people working his own corner. He looked confident, strong, gorgeous, in his jeans and T-shirt, just as he had that night in San Francisco. They had both opted for a more casual look, and again, just like the last time she'd seen him, he looked *damn good.*

He laughed at something a young man said to him, and the sound rang over the din of the packed room. When he looked up, he caught her eye, and they maintained contact for a brief moment, before she turned back to the young woman she was speaking with. She then moved on, making her way through the crowd, until she found herself in front of Rafael.

He looked down at her, his smile amused but cordial, and she nearly blushed at the way secrecy lingered between them. Her own lips tipped upward.

"Hello, Jessica." He turned back briefly to the people

he was talking to. "Excuse me, for a moment." They found a quiet corner.

"Hello," she replied politely. She turned to the crowd, if only in an attempt to not look at him. "Great crowd, huh?"

"Certainly is. Pollsters think voter turnout is going to reach an all-time high."

"I didn't think you listened to the polls," she said, referring to the conversation they'd had at the diner. Maybe he cared more than he let on.

Another flash of white teeth. "You caught me."

"And from what I hear, most of them are going to vote for me." She looked at him to gauge his reaction to the polls that had been released earlier that morning, which had shown her ahead by a couple of points. Nowhere near a landslide, though.

His face remained neutral. If her words had had any effect, he didn't show it. "It's not over until it's over."

"It could be over," she continued to prod at him. "You could just save face and drop out now. Save yourself the embarrassment of being beaten by me."

He looked at her, silent for a moment, before he threw his head back and let loose with a loud laugh. A photographer took the opportunity to take their picture, it probably looked like they were enjoying a cordial joke, but the subtext behind the moment was much heavier.

He leaned over her, close enough to her ear. "I could say the same thing about you. Have you forgotten that I could end your campaign in a second?"

He was right, and she tried not to let her confidence waver. "You wouldn't."

"Are you sure? Maybe I'd do anything to win."

And he would, too. "Go right ahead," she challenged him. "I mean, if you don't think you can beat me fairly on the merit of your campaign, go against your word. You could win in a dirty way if you really want to. But your term as mayor would always have an asterisk next to it."

He raised an eyebrow and smirked at her. "You're good." He changed his stance, moved closer. "I've got to be honest, I've been thinking about you since yesterday."

That caught her off guard. "Really?" It surprised her that she'd left him just as affected as he'd left her. "I've been thinking about you, too." Her voice lowered to a whisper. "I've been especially thinking about whether or not I'd go online and see my picture splashed all over the internet."

"I didn't tell anyone."

"I know."

"Not yet."

Jessica pulled back and frowned. "I don't have time to fool around with you. If you're going to expose me, then just do it."

"But this is too damn fun, don't you think?"

"I'm not having fun." She reconsidered. "Well, I wasn't up until a couple of hours ago."

"Oh, really? What changed?"

"Yeah, you're not the only one with information. I may have unearthed one of those skeletons you spoke of."

"What have you got?"

"Why don't I tell you tonight? I could meet you at Di Terrestres."

His jaw ticked, and his eyes widened slightly. His self-assured mask faltering only for a fraction of a second before glossing over again.

"You know the place?" she asked innocently.

He nodded. "I do. I'm a member, like many people."

"I heard you're a little more than just a member." She smiled when he said nothing. "I thought as much. Why don't you put me on the guest list, and we can talk over all of this?" She was bluffing, expecting him to laugh again and move along. Maybe try to shut her up. But instead he leaned in. She inhaled and involuntarily pulled in more of his spicy cologne.

"Sounds like a good idea to me," he agreed. "Be there at nine."

Jessica nodded. Less than an inch separated their bodies. She was brought back to the cab, sitting on his lap, kissing him, being touched so intimately by him.

"I'm looking forward to it. I know you are, too." He made a point to let his eyes roam over her body. His gaze scorched her skin, and if he didn't stop soon, she was certain her body would start smoking.

"And how do you know that?"

He leaned closer again, and she held her breath, trying not to inhale, lest she pull his expensive cologne or his natural essence into her body. "Because I know that you haven't forgotten about that kiss, and the way I touched you, or the way you pressed your sweet ass into my hard dick in the back of that cab."

Despite herself, she gasped. His sultry words affected her as if he'd touched her. She'd had the upper hand ever so briefly, but in just one sentence he'd taken it back. His grin was knowing. The man had a wicked way about him, and he knew it.

Quickly enough to give her whiplash, he straightened and turned back into the sturdy, serious politician. And he moved away from her. He extended his hand, and she shook it; again, someone took their photo. "I'll see you tonight," he promised, before backing away from her, disappearing into the crowd and allowing her to breathe again.

Gordon, her campaign manager, came up behind her. "Only twenty minutes left," he said. "We should also get together tonight to go over new strategies based on what we learned from people today. What do you think?"

Jessica snapped herself free of Rafael's trance. "Um, tonight?" she stammered. "That doesn't work for me. I have another meeting."

Jessica didn't know what would happen when she arrived at Di Terrestres, but she knew that whatever did would change everything between her and her political rival. While she was apprehensive, part of her was also excited to see Rafael again, and to see what Di Terrestres was really all about.

This was her opportunity. There was nothing wrong with checking it out. The plan that formed in her head was twofold. She could see him again to make sure that he wouldn't go back on his word to reveal her secret. But that wasn't it. Her entire body burned at the thought of the kiss, and she knew that it shouldn't happen again, but there was absolutely no telling that to her libido. She couldn't help but do the mental math of how many days it'd been since she'd had sex, and she lost count. Jessica was a single woman, there was nothing wrong with sex, or seducing a man she wanted, and even though she shouldn't, she wanted Rafael. Maybe she could have her cake and eat it, too.

CHAPTER FIVE

LATER THAT EVENING, on the top floor of the BH, Rafael sat at his desk, trying with all his power to focus on work, while his friends, the rest of the members of The Brotherhood, all occupied their usual table on the bottom floor at Di Terrestres. For what must have been the hundredth time in the past hour, he looked at his watch. The minute hand crawled in its circle. Counting the minutes, seconds, *milliseconds* until it was nine o'clock.

He flexed his fingers and turned back to his computer. His current task was to write a speech for a chamber of commerce event the next day, but all he could focus on was the possibility of Jessica showing up at Di Terrestres that night. In fact, he hadn't even been able to concentrate on anything since seeing her that afternoon. She hadn't promised him anything, but he knew that she would show up. Either way, he'd asked the club's doorman to let him know if, *when*, she arrived.

His office phone rang. And he sighed in frustration.

"Want me to get that?" His assistant, Jillian, looked up from her spot at the large conference table. He'd had it brought into his office to seat his team when they met for their weekly campaign meetings. Jillian was busy scheduling that week's appearances, and clearly wasn't having as much trouble focusing as he was. An invaluable member of his team, she did everything he needed, and he wasn't sure he could make do without her.

"No, it's fine." He picked up the phone. "Rafael Martinez," he said, answering.

"For fuck's sake, you're still in your office?" Alex chided him.

He rolled his eyes. "The fact that you called my office and I responded should give you your answer to that."

"Are you coming down?" he asked. "You abandoned me last night. We're all here. Brett and Rebecca, too, just back from their honeymoon. Come down for a drink."

Rafael wanted to go downstairs. He'd hadn't made time for much fun as of late, but when he looked around at the papers that covered his desk, he didn't know if he could. There were so many more tasks to complete before the next day. "I was hoping to be able to get away," he conceded, not letting on that he'd made a date—*no, not a date*—with Jessica. He exhaled a deep breath. "But I've got a to-do list the length of my arm, and I still have a speech to write for tomorrow."

"You work too hard, you know that, right?" Alex asked him.

"That's rich, coming from you." Rafael chuckled,

knowing his friend worked as many hours as he did. But when Alex played, he played hard.

"If you don't come down, we're coming up," Alex insisted, filling the silence. "You need to get out of the office for once."

"As my campaign manager, shouldn't you be making sure I stay on the straight and narrow?"

"The stick up your ass is already straight and narrow enough for both of us. And I'm off the clock, I'm telling you this as your friend."

Rafael laughed. Alex always did have a way with persuasion. "Okay, fine. Give me thirty minutes. Then I'll be down for one drink. I've got a meeting later."

"With who?"

"None of your concern," he said, before hanging up the phone. When he replaced the receiver in the cradle, he saw that Jillian was watching him.

"Go downstairs," she told him. "You deserve a break. I can finish your speech."

"No—" He tried to refuse.

"You need a break. Go see your friends."

"Thanks." He smiled gratefully. "But you know I like to write my own speeches. And I think you've got your hands full already."

"Well, you know, I'm here to lighten your load."

"And I greatly appreciate it. You're a fantastic help."

"You work too hard."

"I'm starting to hear that quite a bit lately," he muttered. "All right, I'm going to take off for the night. Maybe you should do the same. I'll get up a little earlier, maybe skip the gym, and I'll write my speech in the morning."

"I'll just finish up here, and then I'll go home, too," she told him.

"Okay," he said standing. Maybe he did work too much, but he could also see that Jillian was tired. What he needed to remember was that his workload affected everyone on his team. They all needed a break. "You can let yourself out." He headed for the door, and she waved to him.

"I'll see you tomorrow."

Rafael got into the private elevator that took him from the top floor to the ground floor, where Di Terrestres was located. When the doors opened again, he stepped onto the floor of the club. Rafael looked around, pleased with the number of people who had come by on a Monday night.

The bar took up one entire wall, and world-class mixologists served only the finest of libations. Lush, high-backed booths, banquets and plush couches lined the far wall, and high- and low-top tables were scattered throughout the large room. At the center was a large floor, sometimes used as a dance floor, but mostly used as a stage for the nightly erotically charged shows. Circling the room were beautiful hostesses in short gold dresses, taking drink orders, bringing food and cigars, and arranging special, private accommodations for guests, if needed. On a lower floor were the secret exhibition and demonstration rooms, available only to the most important and discreet clients to explore their secret desires. But the best part of the club, as far as Rafael was concerned, were the luxury bedroom suites for those needing a place to crash for the night, or a little *extra privacy.* They were outfitted for anything a discerning customer might desire. All they had to do was speak to one of the club's concierges and tell them what they needed, and as long as it was safe, consenting and *within reason*, it would be supplied for a price. Despite being open for only a couple years, Di Terrestres was already the group's most profitable venture, and had heavily padded all of their bank accounts.

Rafael walked farther into the club and looked around. He quickly found his friends Alex, Alana, Gabe, Brett and Brett's new wife, Rebecca. *The Brotherhood.* It was a name they'd slyly given themselves, a nod of the hat to the secret societies that many rich and powerful men belonged to. But ironically, it was Alana who had come up with the name one night as a joke, and much to her dismay, it had stuck.

Taking in the room with a sweep of his head, he saw many faces, some personally familiar, others well-known in the public eye. But they all had in common a need for the privacy that existed at Di Terrestres, to live their lives without judgment or the threat of having their kinks and desires made public. While outsiders knew about the club, not many were invited in, and even fewer actually knew what happened behind its closed doors. There were rumors, of course, and suppositions, but thankfully, no one was talking. Guests had to be vetted by the owners—himself and his four friends.

Rolling up his sleeves, Rafael crossed the floor toward the elevated balcony where their regular table was found. The table gave them a full, unobstructed view of the goings-on of their dominion. His friends leaned back in their seats, nursing their drinks and taking in the sights, most likely reveling in the success of the full bar and their other enterprises. He climbed the staircase to their table and sat at the empty seat. Before he could turn his head around to signal a waitress for a drink, one placed a short glass on the table in front of him, which he knew contained his favorite high-end Scotch. "Thank you, Beth," he said. Even though he wasn't behind the staffing at Di Terrestres, that was Alana's job, he tried to make a point of remembering the names and faces of each of the employees.

"No problem, Mr. Martinez."

"That's *Mayor* Martinez," Gabe corrected her with a laugh, his words slurring slightly.

"You're a pain in the ass, Gabe," Alana said, rolling her eyes. "Don't mind him, Beth."

"I don't," she said, before turning her attention back to Gabe. "My mistake, *Mr. Foster*," she said, raising a smart eyebrow at Gabe, putting him in his place.

"That's Mr. Foster, *Esquire*," he told her, with a smile, and they all shared a hearty laugh with Beth before she walked away, her hips swaying, which Gabe watched appreciatively. Rafael glanced around at his friends, whose spirits were high; judging by the empty glasses on the table, the party had long ago started without him.

They were a close-knit group who shared everything. Over time, they'd found each other and discovered they had a lot in common, and ambitious goals. He and Alex had been friends since childhood, when Alex had come to live with his family. They'd met Brett in grade school, then Gabe and Alana in their early twenties during college. Back then they'd been less inclined to party, and were more interested in entrepreneurship, building their portfolios, working hard to achieve their goals. After college, the group figured that they should join forces, develop their businesses and invest the profits in each other. Their current success was a collaborative effort, and Rafael knew he wouldn't have gotten anywhere, in business or in politics, without them. They were his support system, and they kept each other sane when the work piled up. Which it did. Often.

Work was their priority, but that didn't mean they didn't know how to make room for fun. Especially now that they'd about made it in the business sphere. They were still young, rich, good-looking. When work was done for the day, no matter what the hour, they'd often cut loose at the club, unwind with drinks, conversation and often sex.

He took a sip of his Scotch.

"How's the campaigning coming, Mayor?" Gabe asked.

"So far so good, but let's not get too ahead of ourselves," Rafael said. He wasn't superstitious, but he didn't want to tempt fate when it came to the upcoming election. "I'm not quite the mayor yet."

"No, but you're a shoo-in for it," Gabe added. "Thompson basically handpicked you to be his successor."

"Well, you know, that's the funny thing about democracy. It's generally up to the people to decide. Right now, I'm neck and neck with Jessica Morgan." Under the table, Rafael clenched his fists, trying not to let on to the fact that just saying her name affected him in a physical way. "She's completely got the female and the youth votes locked down." He'd spent many hours with his team trying to figure it out. Admittedly, he had no idea how to break into the female demographic, outside of using his good looks and sex appeal, but he didn't want to win like that.

"What's her story, anyway?" Brett asked him.

"I don't know, really. My PI didn't find out anything about her," he muttered into his glass, not liking that he was outright lying to his friends. He met Alex's eyes over the rim of his glass, and he warned his friend not to say anything. Thankfully he didn't.

He noticed when Alana and Rebecca exchanged a skeptical glance. "What wrong?"

"You had her investigated?" Alana asked, incredulous.

"It's not a big deal. I can't beat her if I don't know what I'm up against."

"Still, it sounds kind of shady."

"Politics is shady, perhaps even more than business," he told her. "Don't be naive. This is how it's done. I look into everyone I have dealings with. I like to get all the dirt up so there aren't any surprises."

"Everyone has dirt, though. Even you," Alana reminded him, raising an eyebrow as she looked around the club. He'd hidden his ties to the club, and the rest of the businesses, of which he had an equal piece. His ownership in The Brotherhood's operations was held in a blind trust, with the other members as trustees. It was morally ambiguous, of course, but completely legal. For all intents and purposes, on paper, he had nothing to do with the business, or the management of the combined assets. But as for Di Terrestres, he knew that his affiliation with the ownership of an erotic club would certainly affect his campaign, and political life. So he wasn't officially on the books as an owner, just a guest with a VIP membership.

Rafael shrugged, unbothered by the women's opinions of his actions. "I'm not worried." Although, Jessica had somehow found out about his ownership, or so she'd let on. He checked his watch. Eight forty-five. He looked to the door. Either way, he'd find out in fifteen minutes.

"I don't think you have to worry too much about Jessica Morgan, though. She doesn't have the connections you have," Alex told him. "You're known in this city, you've been a part of the city council for what, ten years, since you got out of college. She came out of nowhere. It'll work out for you. I'm confident."

He wouldn't admit it, but that was what scared Rafael the most—that she had come from nowhere and had already made huge advances in the opinion polls. It was unheard of, running for the top seat, being a virtual newcomer, with just two years of municipal government experience, but the fact that she was making such a huge impact was what made him uneasy. "It's not that simple. I'll worry about every aspect of the campaign until after the election when I'm settling into my new office."

Jessica wasn't a longtime politician. She wasn't schooled like one. She was idealistic and legitimately wanted to help people, and he had to commend her for that. She had pipe dreams of making a difference but no real experience in the matters used to get things done.

The table grew quiet, and he drank from his glass and thought about Jessica. Just as he'd done every night, virtually every minute, since the start of his campaign. But now he knew her. Intimately. He'd kissed her, brought her to orgasm. And his blood stirred as he pictured her on the stage at Charlie's, on his lap in the back of a car in the light of dawn. And he knew he'd affected her today at the student union event.

He blew out a breath and took another sip from his glass, and looked around at his friends. With the exception of Brett, who was whispering in Rebecca's ear, the rest of them consulted the illuminated screens of the phones in their hands. Rafael didn't mind. Everyone at the table understood they weren't being inconsiderate. They were never truly off the clock. Even when they were at Di Terrestres, work never stopped for them. The Brotherhood always had something going on, real estate to develop, deals to make, restaurants and charity organizations to run, a campaign to win.

The lights of the club dimmed, and fire started from the elegant torches on the wall, casting the room in a flickering golden light. Most of the conversation quieted. It was almost nine, and it was the time at night when the mood in the club shifted. Things became less playful and took a serious turn. Couples and groups gathered closer, touching, kissing, extending foreplay, and many left for the suites upstairs or the demo rooms downstairs.

It had been a while since Rafael had taken advantage of the benefits of Di Terrestres. But in the muted, low light, he allowed himself to relax a little, as his gaze fixed on a nearby torch.

The fire, the heat, the sensuality made him think back to Jessica, and the way her touch, her brand burned within him. She was hot, fiery, and he knew that she would burn him deeply. It would be best to stay away from her, but he also knew he wouldn't. He gulped down his Scotch and pulled at the collar of his shirt to cool himself. It didn't work.

His gaze shifted to the door, and as if his desires had brought her into his presence, she appeared in the doorway. She'd shown up. Jessica was in his club.

CHAPTER SIX

Jessica took a deep breath as she signed the digital confidentiality contract on the doorman's tablet, widening her eyes at the protections the club had in place, and she handed it back. Now sworn to secrecy, she again stood outside the dark curtain, shoring her confidence, trying to look cool, while she considered turning on her heel and leaving. But something kept her moving and, as she took a step, another attendant moved the curtain aside. Perhaps it was her stubbornness, but it was most likely the ache in her core. She wanted to pretend that she was there to tell Rafael to go fuck himself, to hold the fact that she also knew his secret over his head. But she knew that wasn't it. There was something more primitive driving her. Something she couldn't control. Something a woman felt for a man.

There was no denying it, Jessica wanted him, and she wouldn't be able to focus on anything else until she had him. She'd already blown off meeting with her campaign manager. What else would she jeopardize for a chance to be with him? God, she didn't want to want him. But there was no other reason for her to go there, to his sex club, if they didn't end their evening with their clothes on the floor.

She tried to tell herself that it was just a precaution, to make sure he wouldn't discuss what he knew about her. Perhaps they could come to an understanding. But the other part of her remembered vividly the way he'd spoken to her that afternoon.

Looking around, she tried to get the vibe of Di Terrestres. The music was a slow, low hip-hop beat, and she almost swayed her hips, losing herself in it before she snapped out of it and realized no one else was dancing. She was surprised by the size of the club. Despite the square footage, through some miracle of design, it still managed to feel intimate and close.

The walls were lined with plush booths, and each held anywhere from two to five people engaged in some sort of romantic entanglement. A long bar ran along the opposite wall. And she beelined for a drink. But on the way, she saw many familiar faces. Colleagues, athletes, celebrities, notable citizens of Las Vegas, voters. At first, she panicked, thinking that they would recognize her, but when they smiled and nodded politely in greeting, they moved on. Finally, she made her way to the bar and ordered merlot. If they wouldn't give her the entire bottle, which was what she actually needed, she would settle with a glass.

Either way, she'd put a seriously long time into getting ready. She'd settled on a simple little black dress and a pair of black leather T-strap heels. And she'd picked out her favorite push-up bra and lace thong combo for underneath. The outfit always made her feel confident and in charge, and she hoped she would still feel that way after seeing him.

She took a sip and looked around, wondering how it was all supposed to work. She was a little early. She couldn't sit at home and count the minutes until nine any longer. She looked around again, wondering if she should go find Rafael. How would he know she was there?

Maybe she'd been stupid. Maybe he was looking to embarrass her. "Why do you look so nervous?" She heard a familiar masculine voice as someone approached her from behind. She turned her head and came face-to-face with Rafael Martinez. "A sensual woman like yourself fits right in with this crowd."

Jessica tried not to tremble at the smooth, deep sound of his voice. "I'm not nervous."

His smile was smug, and she was torn between slapping him and kissing him. He reached out and touched her bottom lip with his thumb, and he leaned in, placing his lips on hers for a brief second. "For a politician, you aren't very good at schooling your emotions."

The contact almost made her sigh, but she controlled herself. "You're pretty full of yourself." The bartender handed him a short glass tumbler that contained an amber liquid, a drink that he hadn't ordered, and he took the seat next to her. He took a sip and then smiled again.

Despite the sultry music, the sexuality that surrounded her, the smell of Rafael's cologne and just how badly she wanted to fuck the man beside her, Jessica had a moment of clarity, one that told her that this wasn't right. She stepped up from the barstool. "You know what, I think I might have made a mistake. I should go." His hand on her forearm stopped her. The same electricity that had coursed between them before still existed, and their eyes locked. "Why don't we just leave it at this? We'll promise to never speak of the other's extracurricular activities, and just forget everything."

"Stay," he said. The command was simple, and his voice was low, but authoritative. And Jessica hated the way she found herself listening to him, taking her seat again, without taking her eyes from his.

"Thank you," he said, sitting back on his barstool.

They both sipped their drinks in silence for some moments, watching the other over the rim of their glasses. "I should have known that you were behind Di Terrestres."

"And what exactly do you know about it?"

She looked around, and her eyes landed on a booth where a man sat with two women, taking turns kissing them between gulps of expensive champagne. "I'd heard of it. I know it's erotic. Some kind of sex club, or something. I've heard there are rooms here somewhere, where wild things happen."

"And here you are, because of it, or regardless of the fact? Are you looking to burn off a little energy, or de-stress?" He glanced around. "That's what a lot of our high-profile guests come here for. I know the campaign's taken a lot out of you."

"How do you know that?"

"You look tense. I can't help but think it might be because of our kiss? Maybe you're here because you need to get laid."

Kiss was a bit of a misnomer for what they'd shared in the back of that cab in San Francisco. "And what if I am?" she whispered and leaned closer to him. "What if I did come here to find some guy to fuck? I think you'd better get out of here, though, and let me find him. I doubt anyone will approach me if you're hanging around."

"Now, why would I just leave and let another man fuck you?"

"Is the fact that I asked you to not enough?"

"If you recall, I *asked you* to invite me up to your hotel room on Saturday night, and you didn't." He reached out and touched her cheek. "So, we have an established history of not doing what the other wants." He paused and leaned closer. "But what if I asked you now to come upstairs with me?"

She sat back away from him and looked around. Her body told her that was what she wanted. But her mind still held out. "What if someone sees us together?"

"It doesn't matter." He reached out for her again and cupped her cheek. "Nobody cares here."

Rafael smiled and nodded over her shoulder, gesturing behind her. She turned to see two men, one a well-known local businessman, the other an entertainer, ascend the staircase to his left. They were holding hands and looking at each other with heat and affection in their eyes.

"Isn't that—" she asked him, after recognizing the couple.

Rafael nodded. "Neither of them is officially out, for whatever reason. That's up to them. But they regularly meet up here. In no other public building in the city would the two of them be able to show open affection. What they do here is on their terms."

"And no one says anything to the press?"

"No. There's no reason for anyone to say anything about what goes on here between consenting adults. Everyone signs the same confidentiality form as you did, and it is as binding as any other legal document. We have a team of lawyers, led by my friend Gabe, who makes sure to enforce it. This is a safe place for all sorts of indulgent behavior. No one here cares who spends time with who, or who goes to bed with who. It's a place where people can be themselves, meet colleagues, talk business, but also act out their most secret fantasies and desires, without fear that they would be outed in their communities. But for the most part, people come here for the same reason, to get away from the public attention that surrounds their usual lives."

It struck true to Jessica. Rafael knew about her secret, but apparently, she wasn't the only one with a secret. She looked around. It made sense to her. If she could somehow live her life the way she wanted, as a world-renowned exotic dancer, and have a life in politics, she would jump at the chance. But she was sure that she could never afford what was most likely a hefty membership fee.

"Come on," he said. "Why don't we go somewhere a little bit quieter?"

It was a couple of beats before she responded, and Rafael wasn't sure whether she would just turn and walk away. She seemed at war with herself but she nodded, a small, nearly imperceptible bob of her head, but he caught it.

She stood and he put his palm on the small of her back, though he let her break away to walk a couple steps ahead of him. Then he escorted her up the staircase that led to his private room. While his friends had bedrooms in their offices, Rafael did not, opting instead to use the extra space for work purposes. Instead he'd chosen one of the suites as his own private sanctuary. Additionally, he didn't want to sleep in the same place where he worked, recognizing the importance of separating work from his regular life.

His heart pounded in his chest, and he couldn't hear anything but the *bud-um* in his ears. As Jessica walked, she seemed oblivious to the way he couldn't keep his eyes from the sway of her hips underneath her dress. He was transfixed by the way the movement made the material fall against her thighs, highlighting the body that he'd seen, touched, the weekend before.

He caught up and casually dropped his hand on her hip, stopping her in front of the door to his own suite. He felt her eyes on him as he swiped his key card to unlock the door. When he heard the heavy metal clink of the lock, he opened the door and stepped back so she could enter in front of him.

The motion sensor on the lights activated and the room filled with a low, muted glow, reminiscent of candlelight. The room was small, comfortable and held minimal furniture, just an armoire and a large king-size bed, which was flanked by modern nightstands. A door on the opposite wall was ajar. It led to a bathroom that contained a stand-up shower. There was also a fully stocked mini-fridge, and a small wet bar.

She laughed—not the reaction he was expecting. When she turned to speak to him, one of her eyebrows was cocked inquisitively.

"What's so funny?"

"I've been so stupid."

"What makes you say that?"

"My secret could destroy my career and my reputation, but people wouldn't even bat an eye at your—*what is this?*—your secret sex room?"

"It's not a secret sex room." He chuckled, walked to the minibar and picked up a bottle of wine. "Cabernet sauvignon?" he asked. She nodded, and he poured them each a glass and brought her one. When she accepted it, their fingers touched. A shock of static snapped between them, and when their eyes locked, he knew she'd felt it, too. She pulled away quickly and brought her glass to her lips.

"Why do you have a bedroom in your nightclub? If it isn't for seduction?"

"It sometimes gets used for seduction," he admitted with an easy smile. "But, the more boring answer is that I spend a lot of my nights here when I'm working. My office is on the top floor of the building."

"You have an office here, too? Besides the one in city hall?"

"I do, but I like my office here better. I got to design it, it's comfortable and has all the amenities I could need, and the luxuries I don't want, or expect, the taxpayers to pay for. It's also my campaign headquarters. So, you can imagine how important it is to have a place to sleep nearby."

Jessica eyed him, as if she could see right through him. "There's more, isn't there? I was able to find out that you're an owner in this place. You still have ownership in your businesses, don't you?"

She was good.

When he didn't respond, she smirked. "Isn't that a conflict of interest, Councillor?"

He stiffened. She was questioning him, and he knew that it would come back to haunt him if he let her get too close to his operations. While he knew her secret, he didn't want her to know too much about him. "I still intend to maintain a part-ownership of the businesses, but in a more limited scope. My interests are in a blind trust, so I don't have any say in how the assets are managed." It was true, and she couldn't refute the legality of the arrangement.

"And how do you think voters would respond to your ownership in an erotic club? One of the sexiest clubs in the city. I've heard some rumors about the things that go on behind closed doors."

"And that's exactly why we keep the doors closed." He grinned. "Honestly, not many people know about my affiliation with the club. I'm not officially on the books as an owner, in fact, I'm not quite sure how you found out." He wondered if her PI was possibly as good as his own... "But I'm still part of the partnership. So the voters? They probably wouldn't like it. But Di Terrestres is like any other type of social club. Our clients can come here and mingle without having to worry about being caught in a compromising position. There's no press, no outsiders. Just a safe space and like-minded people living out their secret fantasies."

"So tell me, what kinds of things happen here?"

Rafael folded his arms across his chest. "I'll take this time to remind you of the nondisclosure agreement you signed when you walked in the door. You can't use any of this against me during the campaign. Our lawyers will be all over you in seconds. And they're good, worth every penny. There's no way you could beat us."

"I won't tell anyone. But I hope that means you can keep my secret, as well?"

He knew then that he would, but he wouldn't say so, and went on with the introduction of the club. "People can mingle or dance in the main room, where we also have shows. Things can get pretty hot and heavy in there. And we also host dinners and a semiannual masquerade ball." She nodded, and he held her rapt attention as he told her about the exhibition rooms, the concierge service and finally about the privacy suites where they were now.

She looked around the room. "And you bring women up here?"

"I have."

"Why did you bring me? If you want to *talk*, why aren't we talking in your office? Is that not quiet enough?"

"You're a smart woman. I don't think I have to explain why I brought you up here. I want you. And I haven't been able to stop thinking about you since San Francisco."

"I've been thinking about it, too."

One corner of his mouth ticked upward. "I know. And I know you don't want to go to my office, either. You're right where you want to be."

They sipped their wine silently.

"What are we doing here?" Her question was rhetorical, and she shook her head. "This is such a bad idea."

"I've had worse ideas," he told her. "I told you why I invited you up here tonight. Now tell me this, why did you come here tonight?" He wanted to hear the words. Judging from her body language, the way she turned toward him, the outfit she'd chosen, the way her eyes roamed over him, he knew exactly why she'd come to him.

"I wanted to hold it over your head that I know your secret." He looked unconvinced and she hesitated. "I've just been kind of edgy all day."

"Edgy?" he asked, scooting a little closer to her on the couch.

She turned to face him, and drawing a seductive line over her upper lip with her tongue, she smiled. "What if I said I was horny?"

He raised an eyebrow. "Oh, yeah?"

She nodded. "Maybe you were right, I just have all of this anxious tension. I guess it's the debate coming up. Everything with the campaign." She turned to face him more fully, and her voice dropped lower. "You feel it, too."

"I do," he said. He wanted nothing more than to kiss her. He'd craved her flavor for days. He leaned in, and when his lips were only millimeters from sampling hers, she pulled back.

"Wait." She sat back, putting distance between them.

"What's wrong?"

"Nothing." She shook her head. "I don't know. I just need to think."

"I want you. And I thought you wanted me. What's there to think about?"

"It's not that simple. There's the campaign to think about."

"That's where you're wrong. There's really nothing more simple, basic or primal than what we want. *Desire*. It's not rational, it doesn't have to involve thinking." He traced a finger down her arm. "Just go with it. We can worry about everything else tomorrow. It doesn't have to change anything, and we can go back to hating each other tomorrow."

"You promise?" She laughed. "*Just go with it.* I like the sound of that."

Rafael finished the rest of his drink in one fortifying gulp, then poured himself another serving of wine. He turned back to her. "Want some more?" he asked, proffering the bottle.

She noticed her glass was empty and nodded, holding it out.

Rafael had brought Jessica up to his suite to have his way with her. He'd wanted it on his terms, as always. But he realized it wouldn't be that easy. When he sat back down, it was on the opposite end of the couch, to give her some space.

"So, what are you thinking?" he asked.

Jessica said nothing. He could tell that her mind was still racing. She was thinking too damn much.

Rafael watched her, confused by her but trying not to let it show. She took her bottom lip between her teeth again, just as she had when he'd seen her walk into the club. The move, while it turned him on, also made her look small and vulnerable. He knew she was anything but.

"I still think this is a bad idea," she told him, but she scooted closer to him on the couch, making up for the space he'd made.

"I know it is," he agreed. He sat only an inch away from her now, and with every deep breath that Jessica took, the rise and fall action caused her breasts to graze his chest. He didn't care about anything else, he only knew that at that moment, in the present, giving in to this overwhelming connection outweighed the damage or repercussions it would have on his future. He would worry about those later. "But it seems kind of inevitable, don't you think? Just based on our chemistry. We're helpless against it."

"For one night, we could put it all away, and just be two people who are physically attracted to each other, and just relieve some of the tension. Because we'd both be lying to ourselves if we denied that there was anything between us." She looked down at the bulge in his lap. Putting her wineglass on the end table and then her hand high on his thigh, she stroked him, his muscles hard through the material of his pants. "Judging from that—" she nodded at the bulge in his lap "—I can see that you agree."

Jessica's fingers were like heated knives moving up and down his leg, and he tried to swallow past the lump that desire had formed in his throat. He'd never felt so perplexed by a woman. Jessica would be a challenge for him.

"But let's be clear," she said. "I just want sex. This doesn't mean that I like you."

He laughed. He wasn't entirely sure if he liked her, either. But he respected her, and he wanted her. "Well, I guess I'll just have to take that, then."

CHAPTER SEVEN

THE GROWL IN his throat was all Jessica knew before Rafael lifted her from her place on the couch and pulled her into his lap. His lips took hers in a kiss so powerful it stole her breath, and his tongue pushed into her mouth and was molten as it found hers and stroked it. He leaned back and moved from under her, flipping them before dropping to his knees on the floor in front of the couch. He reached up her skirt and pulled down her panties, roughly yanking them down her thighs and over her ankles before tossing them over his shoulder.

"There's been something on my mind since Saturday night," he told her, looking up as he positioned himself between her knees.

She stiffened. "And what's that?"

"That I touched you, but I still have no idea how your pussy tastes."

Without an ounce of pretense, Rafael grabbed her ass and pulled her to him, her legs spreading to him, and without warning, his mouth was on her, hot and wet, as his lips closed over her crease. His tongue snaked between her folds, and his groan of approval as he tasted her vibrated throughout her entire body.

That devilish tongue spread her open to him, each of her nerve endings exposed to his mouth, and he knew right where to touch, and how to make her lift her hips from the couch to get closer to him. He used his lips, tongue, even teeth, making her body tighten in response to the delicious onslaught. When she didn't think she could handle it, he inserted two fingers, curling them, so he hit her G-spot just right. Clearly the man knew what he was doing.

"Oh, fuck," she whimpered, throwing her head back and pushing her hips against him, desperate for more. His oral ministrations made her crazy as he worshipped her, before her on his knees, winding her tight, more and more, until she found it difficult to breathe, to move, to see. She was on the verge of what she could tell would be an incredible orgasm. "Oh, God, Rafael," she whispered, almost a breath, unable to form actual words and project them audibly.

With his mouth still on her, and not willing to relinquish his hold, Rafael looked up at her. His dark eyes were black with passion, but the sides crinkled with humor, and the knowledge that he was doing an excellent job. She barely noticed when his other hand shifted and one of his fingers moved around to the back, cupping her ass, holding her to him. He stayed the course, however, his eyes open, watching her, taking in her reaction as her breath stuttered in her throat. Each stroke of his fingers and lave of his tongue wound her further, pulled her tighter, but with his lips wrapped around her clit, two fingers inside of her and another pressing along the crevice of her ass, she couldn't take it any longer, and like the tightest coil, she snapped. Throwing her head against the back of the couch, she came with a white flash behind her eyes and a loud scream. Her entire body tensed and strained, and she grasped the back of his head, holding him in place, moving her hips back and forth, using his mouth and chin and fingers to ride out her orgasm and further her own pleasure. He groaned against her flesh, and the sound reverberated throughout her body. And she was hit with another tremor, as additional waves of pleasure lapped over her.

Rafael disengaged from her and in one quick movement, he had her lying, fully supine on the couch, and he was over her. Without realizing it, she had wrapped her legs around his hips, holding him in place, her thighs bracketing him. She caught her breath, but realized that his was just as quick and wavering as hers.

"Christ, Jessica," he moaned in her ear. She could still feel his erection pressing into her behind. "That was so fucking beautiful. You taste so goddamn sweet."

"You're telling me." She felt sated, exhausted, limbless, as he kissed her, and she tasted herself on his lips. He wiped his mouth and chin free of the glistening juices and he licked the edge of his hand with a satisfied groan, gathering the taste on his tongue.

One side of his lips quirked upward. "You ready for more?"

She nodded distractedly, still trying to come down from the rush of endorphins from her previous orgasm.

His chuckle was deep and hearty. She closed her eyes and savored the sound of it.

His palms found her breasts, and he squeezed. She gasped, and pushed her chest into his hands, urging him to play with her nipples. The stiff, needy peaks protruded through her lace bra and dress. Her collar was high and she could feel his impatience with her clothing. He ducked his head and trapped one of her turgid nipples between his lips, and Jessica cried out and watched him as his tongue flicked the bud through the material. If his mouth stoked her fire so hot through her dress, she had no idea how she would survive the contact with her skin. His touch, his taste, his smell, was more potent, more forceful than she could have imagined.

He pulled away briefly, his breath jagged, and they were both transfixed on the wet spot his mouth had left on her chest. "God," he breathed. "I wanted to take my time with you," he told her, his lips on her throat. He smoothed his mouth over her neck, her face, her lips. The stubble of his five o'clock shadow scratched against her skin like sandpaper, and a shock of electricity shot through her and went straight to her core. He took her mouth in yet another bruising kiss, which she wholly reciprocated. Giving as much as she was taking. He breathed life into her, lighting her up inside and sending crackling energy to every nerve ending.

He pulled her dress over her head and snapped the clasp of her bra, freeing her breasts, and she was naked below him and he took great advantage. She wanted to experience all that hot, hard muscle. Her fingers scrambled for the buttons of his shirt and she haphazardly undid them, almost ripping them, clawing at the material. She untucked the shirt from his waistband, and all her hard work was rewarded by his broad chest and shoulders. Rippling muscles underneath smooth, dark skin, with soft black hair that covered his chest and trailed down his rigid abdomen. He was marvelously built.

"Like what you see?"

"Do I ever," she said, before he returned to her.

He grabbed her ass again and pulled her to him, and she could feel the stiff column of his cock against her naked pussy. She wriggled closer, and even though she'd already had one orgasm, she was shameless and desperate to feel him again.

"I know that we're just a few feet from an actual bed," he whispered against her skin. "But if you can feel how hard my cock is, then you know that I can't wait one more second."

Feeling playful, Jessica reached down and grabbed the bulge over the taut material of his gray pants. She squeezed, and he shuddered, growling a low feral sound in her ear.

"I feel it," she said with a moan, still grasping him. He felt huge in her hand, and she wanted him, just as much as he seemed to want it. "And I want it inside of me."

"Jesus," he muttered, looking down at her, while he

still held her wrists in place. She was trapped by him and she couldn't have gotten away if she wanted to. He unbuckled his belt, unzipped his pants and then reached back to his pocket. He pulled out his wallet, withdrew a foil-wrapped condom and threw the leather billfold on the end table above her head. She was amazed by the number of things the man could do with just one hand, and she bit her lip when he raised the condom packet to his mouth and tore it open with his teeth.

She watched riveted as he lowered his pants and boxers, and watched his cock spring free, released from the tensile material. Her breath caught. He was huge, and perfect, and he was ready for her. A drop of pre-cum hung from the tip, and she licked her lips desperate for a taste. A fleeting moment of regret told her that she wouldn't get that opportunity—this was strictly a one-shot deal. She watched as he rolled the latex over his length and grabbed her hips, aligning her with him.

In one powerful thrust, he was inside her. Jessica cried out and closed her eyes. She threw her head back, taking him with her entire body as the sensation of having him fill her overtook her. His groan was loud in her ear as he pulled back and sank deeply into her again. And she gasped, surprised, when he stood and picked her up, gripping the backs of her thighs. Her eyes widened as he used his upper body strength to lift her, then lower her, then lift again, impaling her with his cock, using her body to get himself off. She'd never experienced anything like it. He was so strong, so powerful. He possessed so much control that she would have been amazed by it, if she wasn't so consumed by how good it felt.

He lowered her to the bed and followed, still inside of her. He didn't miss a beat. He kept his steady pace, his rhythm never straying from the percussive way he brought his hips to hers, pushing into her and withdrawing. His eyes never left hers, their connection strong and unending.

Jessica felt her entire body tighten, and her thighs gripped his torso as the pump of his hips became quicker and more frantic. Warmth spread throughout her body and she tossed her head to the side and cried out in release, just as he yelled out an expletive-laced chant. He stilled on top of her, supporting his weight on his elbows, his lips grazing the pulse point below her jaw, as his breath heated her already molten blood.

"Jesus," he whispered. "That was good."

"Oh, my God," she whispered back, barely able to make a sound. Yet somehow she managed to push herself up on the bed, so that she was sitting next to him.

He passed over her wineglass and she accepted gratefully, holding it with still-shaking fingers. She brought the glass to her lips and took a large gulp, which drained the glass. His chuckle was low, devastatingly lustful. "Want some more?"

"Are you talking about the wine?" she asked, knowing that if he was talking about his body, there was no way she could say no.

"I was, yeah," he said, standing. She marveled at

how he could use his legs when hers were jelly. "Unless you're ready for another round."

"I'm not so certain I can move right now," she admitted. She frowned when he reached for his pants, beginning to hide his magnificent body. "You know, I'll bet if you just showed up to the debate naked, it would be a lock for you."

He laughed. "Oh, I don't know. If I showed up naked, you would have to, as well, just to level the playing field, and then I wouldn't be able to focus on anything. Thus, ensuring your victory."

"Ah, you saw through my plan, I guess." She laughed, and then began gathering her clothes. Pulling up her dress, she saw that he was watching her. "What?"

"Still feeling that tension?"

Yes. "Nope." She smiled. "All the tension's gone. You?"

"All spent." He smiled as he buttoned his shirt and looked up at her again. "Do you like me yet?"

She shook her head, but she smiled. "Nope. But you're really good in bed."

He smiled, too. "Well, it's a start, I guess. Maybe we'll have to get together again."

"Yeah, we will," she agreed. "Tomorrow night," she said, heading for the door. "At the debate."

"Tomorrow night," he said, as she opened it and left without saying goodbye.

CHAPTER EIGHT

THE NEXT DAY, Rafael was still a ball of tension as he rode to city hall in the back of his town car. Normally he'd drive himself, but he wanted the extra time to study his notes for that night's debate. Yet as he found himself staring at his notes, he couldn't even think about the debate. He'd lied to Jessica, the night before. None of the tension he'd felt every time she crossed his mind had been spent. Instead, since the night before, it had increased tenfold. His night with Jessica had done nothing to ease him. He was a fidgety mess. Even as he'd pulled out of her, he'd wanted her again, and he'd had to get dressed quickly before he took her again.

With almost every other sexual encounter he'd ever had, he'd been able to put it away, move on and get focused back on the work. But with Jessica, he still wanted her, more than he had before. The only difference being that now he had the privilege of knowing just how incredibly sexy she was, how soft but muscular and lean her body was. He knew the noises she made, the way her body tensed when she came, how smooth her skin was. He shook his head, trying his best to clear the image of her from his head, but he was unsuccessful.

His driver slammed on the brake and Rafael heard the man mutter under his breath at the car that had just cut them off in morning traffic.

Rafael stared down at his notes and was so wrapped up in his thoughts, he didn't even noticed that they had stopped outside city hall. He gathered his things together, and when he exited the car, he pulled his jacket strategically over his lap, to cover the growing erection that just thoughts of Jessica managed to conjure.

He made it two steps into the lobby of the building before his assistant, Jillian, appeared at his side, holding her usual tablet and gigantic purse. The bag always seemed to carry any items either of them could ever need—gum, water bottles, protein bars, pens, notepads, pain meds, spare socks and everything in between.

"Rafael, how is your morning going?" she asked him, falling into step next to him, as they made their way to his office together.

"Pretty well so far, given that it's only 9:00 a.m. Yours?"

"Same. How are you feeling about the debate tonight?"

"Great."

"You're well rested? Hydrated?" she asked, pulling a bottle of sparkling water from her purse and handing it to him.

He swallowed a laugh and accepted it. "Thanks."

She dug into the oversize bag again. "I took the opportunity to make you a few more notes for tonight. And here are your messages, mail and your interdepartmental memos," she told him, withdrawing the stack and passing it over. "Want me to go through it all, let you know what's there and I can respond accordingly?"

"No. I appreciate the offer, but I should handle it." Rafael took the stack; he liked to deal directly with his constituents and colleagues on his own. How could he do the work for the people if he didn't know them?

"And you should also know, Jessica Morgan's gained more points in the latest polls, since that interview she did Friday night. She's really courting the women and the youth vote. You really should consider getting out there in front of the press more. Get your message out."

"My message is out. I don't need to grovel for votes on late-night news," he told her as he unlocked the door to his office, and when she made a step to enter, he turned, blocking her from entering with his body. She was a fantastic assistant, invaluable, even, but sometimes, he just needed his space. "Jillian, I just need a couple of minutes, to ease into my day."

She didn't even falter, not at all put off by him. "Of course. Just buzz me if you need anything."

Rafael walked into his office and shut the door behind him. His city hall office wasn't as comfortable or opulent as his office at the BH. But it was fine. It was more real to him, more modest, humble. It made him feel on the level of the people, not high above them in a tower that dotted the skyline.

Throwing the stack of messages on his desk, he sat

and flipped through them. The last was an envelope. It had been sent to his office, through intraoffice mail from within the building, and was devoid of a return address. He raised an eyebrow as he opened the envelope and removed the single sheet of paper. It was a handwritten message.

Put up your dukes. I'm going to destroy you tonight. -J

He laughed. Ignoring the rest of the messages that required his attention, he pulled out a piece of stationery and wrote his own message to her. Satisfied with his response, he sealed it into an envelope and put it aside to send to her later, before going on with his day.

Just a few doors down from Rafael, Jessica sat in her modestly appointed office and did her best to not slam her forehead on the desk. While she'd made a good show of being composed as she'd written the memo to him, her stomach roiled as she realized how stupid it had been to even go to Rafael's club, let alone to go to his room. He was too slick, too suave, too sexy, too masterful. He'd played her body like a musical instrument, and she'd hummed the right chords for him. But it was such a mistake. He could ruin her campaign, her life—not to mention her panties—in one fell swoop, and she had to stay away from him. She couldn't afford the distraction. And she couldn't afford for him to have all the power.

She turned back to her computer, preparing for the upcoming debate, trying her best to focus her attention on the task at hand—winning. She reviewed current issues that were affecting the people of Las Vegas, even looked at social media to see what people were approving of and complaining about, and then she formulated her talking points. She also had to guess what Rafael's counterpoints would be, which was difficult when the thought of him made her pulse quicken. She'd barely slept last night after their encounter.

There was a knock on her door and Ben walked in, carrying several large paper bags. "I noticed you left your lunch behind, so I grabbed something to make sure you eat. I figured you wouldn't have time for dinner tonight anyway."

She smiled her thanks. "What's on the menu?"

"Sandwiches from that place that just opened not far from here." He looked at the bags in his hands. "But I might have ordered too much. I hope you're hungry."

Her stomach rumbled. "I am, because I also skipped breakfast."

"You have to look after yourself, because you need the energy to beat Mr. Moneybags."

There was another knock on the door, and Gordon walked in. "There's a message here for you." She accepted the envelope and Gordon left. She opened it and almost choked on her coffee when she read the note inside. It was Rafael's retort to her saucy memo earlier.

That's rich, coming from a woman who must have had trouble walking this morning. But after thinking about last night, my dukes aren't the only things that are up.

-R

"Are you okay?" Ben asked, passing her a bottle

of water. He took the paper from her while she drank. "What is this?" he read. "Who's R?" She cringed when the realization dawned on him. "Wait! Rafael Martinez? Jessie, what did you do?"

"Dude, I did something really stupid. I don't even know how it happened."

He didn't look up, and she knew he was rereading the note. "Does this *something stupid* happen to be tall, dark and sexy?"

She didn't respond, and an annoying smirk crossed his face. He saw right through her. "Jessie! Tell me everything!"

Jessica sighed. "Well, it started Friday night, he showed up at the club in San Francisco, looking for me."

"How did he know you were there?"

"I have no idea. He wouldn't tell me." And she had just realized that he'd *never* told her how he'd found out. It still didn't sit right with her, and she couldn't shake it.

"Okay, go on," Ben prodded, already riveted.

Jessica told him the whole sordid tale. From Rafael showing up, their conversation in the diner, the kiss, to her showing up at Di Terrestres and the mind-blowing sex they'd had.

When she finished, Ben sat back in his chair, fanning himself. "Oh, my God," he muttered. "That good, huh?"

Burying her head in her hands, Jessica groaned. "*Incredible!* It was so stupid. I don't even know why I did it. It's like around him, I don't have any free will. I just turn into a quivering bundle of nerves and hormones." The words flew from her mouth and she was unable to staunch them. When she quieted, Ben was watching her, his shocked eyes wide.

"Do you like him?" he asked, suspicion tinging his voice.

"No," she answered quickly.

"No?"

"I don't know. He's sexy, and incredible in bed, but he's still the same arrogant, bullheaded man he was before. And he's my only opponent in the race. Last night was a one-time deal. Let's not forget the fact that at any moment he could tell the world I'm a stripper." Her mind worked overtime to come up with reasons not to like the man. But she no longer worried too much that he would spill her secret. She also had leverage over him. He was part-owner of an erotic club. No matter what he said about her, or how crazy it made her, it didn't erase that fact.

"You have to debate him tonight," Ben said, passing the memo back to her. "So, what are you going to do?"

"I'm going to beat him."

CHAPTER NINE

RAFAEL STOOD ACROSS the stage from Jessica. The lights were bright on them, and Jessica had proven herself a worthy opponent. She'd been prepared and ready for him at every turn. He was impressed, and if she hadn't been his competition, he would have been damn proud of her. The audience had been responsive the entire night. Sometimes they'd been with him, but judging from the reactions in the room throughout, they seemed to side more often with Jessica. The one constant through the entire debate was that behind his podium, his dick was rock hard. Sparring with Jessica, it seemed, turned him on just as much as kissing her did.

"...and sure, Councilman Martinez has a lot of great ideas for ways to stimulate business growth and lower the crime rate, but what's missing from his platform is an identification of the key causes at the root of the problem—poverty and inequality." Jessica looked at him. "Councilman, what is your plan for helping the lower-income families in this city?"

Rafael glared at her. And she returned one that almost made him groan. Thank God for the podium in front of him, because even having her angry at him was an immense turn-on. "My plans for investing in business and infrastructure will target those roots, by providing jobs and making sure people find help when they need it. I have many plans for helping the people who need it—"

"You don't even know who *the people* are," she interrupted, almost yelling. "It's no secret you're in the top 1 percent in this city. You don't know what it's like for the single parents, the unemployed and underemployed."

"Councillor Morgan, Councillor Martinez," the moderator interrupted. "We'll ask you to not address each other directly."

But Jessica carried on, ignoring him. "I've seen the struggle firsthand. I'm on the front lines with community groups. Do you know what it's like to be a woman, working sixty-hour weeks at three separate jobs, and still just managing to scrape by, to put food on the table for her family, or pay for childcare? Have you taken the time to meet her, because I have. My mother was her. I see her every time I walk into one of our centers or outreach centers. Can I ask if you have any idea how many people are just a medical emergency or a car breakdown away from losing everything?"

Rafael looked down at the audience, saw the angry faces nodding along with Jessica's impassioned tirade. "You tell him, girl," he heard a disembodied voice come from the audience, along with several other noises of agreement.

He was losing this. He turned back to face Jessica. The moderator had long since given up on trying to restore order. "I don't know what it's like to be that woman. And yes, I have been extremely successful in my business ventures, but my success came about because of hard work. I was nothing before, and I've worked for everything I have. Don't for a second believe that I don't know struggle. My parents immigrated to America from Mexico when I was a child, looking for a better life. But they worked hard. They achieved their own American dream and they provided a comfortable, but not at all luxurious, life for myself and my sisters. But the one lesson they taught me was that if you work hard, you can achieve anything you want. I work my fingers to the bone every day for myself and my family. And I'm prepared to do the same for the people of this city." When he finished, there was applause, but one look at Jessica told him that she wasn't convinced.

"That's nice," she started. "And I'm glad that you and your family found a better life in this country. But sometimes it isn't enough to work hard. Do you believe that woman I mentioned isn't working hard if she isn't able to live in some penthouse at the top of an ivory tower? That's not always enough. Sometimes, everyone needs a hand, and based on your platform, which doesn't devote itself to the social assistance programs many people rely on, you don't recognize that."

And with that the audience exploded in applause. Rafael was thrown. He'd never received anything but praise in the political arena. He'd always used reason, had always been composed and in control, but Jessica, and her passion, had completely bested him.

"You say I don't know the people of Las Vegas? I've spent every day of the past ten years working for them. Where have you been?" he asked her, frustrated, before turning back to the audience. He knew exactly where Jessica had been, taking off her clothes onstage, and he had had to bite his tongue to stop himself from saying as much. "Ms. Morgan has only been a member of the city council for two years. She's new to politics, she's untested, there's a huge difference in being a citizen, a councilwoman, and the mayor, and I don't think she's up for the transition. But I am, and I'm here to get the job done."

"Councilman Martinez says he's been here for ten years." She turned to him. "What have you done? In your time here, your efforts, along with your platform, are focused on helping business owners and bringing in tourism dollars. As mayor, if you put as much time into helping the people as you did generating wealth, Las Vegas would only then be in great hands."

Rafael's jaw clenched. Jessica knew too much about him. He regretted letting her get so close the night before. While he knew her secret, she also had knowledge that was dangerous to him. "There's nothing wrong with being successful," he told her. His efforts *did* help people. The Brotherhood's ventures had created jobs, and new business was good for the local economy. But he faltered in expressing himself because he knew the crowd was already on her side. There was nothing he could do to bring it back around. It was best for him to not lose his cool. He straightened his shoulders and tried to get the debate back on track, looking pointedly at the moderator to lead them forward.

When the debate, the bloodbath, was finally over, Rafael stepped aside so Jessica could leave the stage first, taking a deep breath as she passed, pulling her scent to him. She was wearing her usual perfume, the one he remembered from the night before, and his body clenched in response. He couldn't remember ever being so prone to sudden erections since he'd left puberty. But Jessica brought it out in him, at extremely inconvenient times.

She didn't even turn back to look at him as he fell in line behind her. And he continued pace, several steps back, trying not to notice the sway of her hips, and he scowled, angry. Rafael didn't need a pollster to tell him that he'd lost the debate. That Jessica had bested him. She'd gotten under his skin, made an impassioned plea to the people. But, dammit, as frustrated as he was he wanted her again. Battling with her onstage was the best kind of foreplay, every bit a better aphrodisiac than the finest champagne and oysters. She was fiery, passionate, intelligent, articulate, and he knew that she wanted to be mayor just as much as he did.

Jessica turned the corner and went toward her office. Rafael didn't look in her direction, nor did he break step as he continued down the hall toward his own office a few doors down.

But he didn't go in.

Stopping in place, he turned his head, and noticing that he was alone in the hallway, he turned back and knocked twice, hard, on her door.

"Come in," she called.

When he opened the door and she saw it was him, she frowned. She must have been expecting someone else. "What do you want?"

He closed the door and walked farther into the room. "To congratulate you on winning the debate."

She busied herself with typing something on her laptop, and he wondered if she was just trying to keep from looking at him. "We don't know that I've won yet."

"You know, I'm kind of impressed," he said. "You made me look awful out there. The way you twisted my words, maybe you are cut out for politics, after all."

"That's the difference between us," she told him. "I'm not playing politics here. I legitimately want to help people."

"And you don't think that's what I want?"

"You certainly have the money and resources to. But you guys built a luxury sex club instead of a playground or a clinic."

He then realized that she had the wrong idea about him. "We donate to charities through our foundation. Just because you don't see it doesn't mean we don't help. We're just not into slapping our names on things."

She said nothing for a moment. But when she spoke again, she looked at him head-on. "But you're a role model in this city. You should be showing people, especially other affluent businesspeople, how much good they can do in helping the little guy."

He thought about that. She had a point. Maybe The Brotherhood could talk more publicly about the things they did with their foundation.

After a poignant silence, she looked up at him, and he could tell that she was tired. "What can I do for you, Councilman?" she asked, using his title. "Why are you here?"

She might be tired, but that didn't mean he wasn't going to goad her. "Councilman? That's awfully formal, isn't it? Considering I was inside of you last night."

Even though she tried to hide it, he saw the shiver that rolled through her. "Well, we're at work now, not at Di Terrestres experiencing the slightest moment of weakness."

He took a step closer, the memories of the way she tasted taking over. "Well, how do you feel about another moment of weakness?" He took another step closer to her. And he caught the way her breath was shaking in and out of her in hurried little gasps. He knew that it was a stupid move. He knew her secret, but in one move she could also destroy his career, his life and everything he'd worked for. The future mayor of the city couldn't be affiliated with a club like Di Terrestres, nor the open lifestyle it promoted. But neither could an exotic dancer, and one of them had to win. It was a benefit to them both to keep all their secrets.

He reached out and pulled her up to him. His lips crashed down onto hers. Unlike their first kiss, or any the night before, this time she didn't stiffen, and her arms encircled his neck and pulled him closer. "Did that fight turn you on as much as it did me?"

"Yeah," she whispered, before pulling him back to her. Kissing him again.

The kiss was rough, savage, and he wanted more. He pushed her against her desk, and lifted her so that her ass perched on the very edge. He kissed her deeply, but she put her palms on his chest and pushed him away. "Rafael, we can't. Especially not here."

"I know," he whispered against her lips. "It's another bad idea."

She nodded, and he could tell she was out of breath. "It wouldn't be our first."

"And probably won't be the last," he promised, dropping to the floor on his knees, before her parted thighs. He needed to taste her again, he was addicted. He leaned into her, spreading her legs farther, bringing him within a hair's breadth of her pussy. Only a thin layer of pink satin separated him from it.

He opened his mouth and his lips closed over her mound, tasting her, inhaling her through her panties. He hooked his thumbs underneath the bands of her underwear, and she obliged him by raising her hips so that he could pull them down over her thighs and let them hang over one of her stiletto-clad feet. He grasped her ass, pulled her core to him and snaked his tongue along her seam, not parting her lips.

She gasped at his touch, and he was satisfied, knowing that he would be responsible for her making many more sounds in the near future. He delved deeper, washing his lips and tongue over her, parting her, finding her wet and hot, ready for his attention. He made several passages over her, coming closer and closer to the sensitive nub of her clit without actually touching it. He could tell by the way she writhed under him that he was driving her crazy. Finally, he flattened his tongue over her clit, and she cried out. He kept one hand on her hip, keeping her still, but he used the other hand, inserting two fingers inside of her, as he closed his lips over her clit. This time, her cry was loud.

He grinned against her, and went to work, fucking her with his fingers, taking her slick flesh into his mouth, sucking, licking, tasting her. She was as delicious as she'd been yesterday, and he feasted. He kept going until she fisted her hand in his hair and thrusted her hips against him, sliding herself against his mouth, taking what she wanted, chasing her own orgasm. He held her in place and maintained a steady pace until she shook under his mouth, and she came with a loud cry.

When her movements quieted, he kept his hands on her thighs, keeping them spread, and he stood between them. He knew her wetness covered his mouth and chin, but he moved in for a kiss without wiping it away. Jessica received his kiss without hesitating, and their tongues danced and dueled as he reached into his back pocket for his wallet. He found it and withdrew a condom hurriedly. Then, without pulling his mouth from hers, he unzipped his pants and took himself in hand.

As if they were victims of the best or worst timing, there was a knock on the door. It caught both of their attention. Jessica looked panicked. And despite the way his entire body screamed out in protest, he stepped away from her and zipped his pants again as she hopped down from the desk and rounded it.

"Come in," she called, straightening her clothes, trying her best to look composed.

A man walked in and went right to Jessica. He wrapped his arms around her waist and lifted her in a hug. "Baby girl, you were amazing!"

Rafael felt a flash of jealousy surge through him. Who was this guy? Why did he have his hands on his Jessica? *His?* He had no idea where that thought had come from. He cleared his throat, reminding them of his presence.

They both looked over at him. "Oh, Ben, this is Councilman Martinez," she said, and Rafael could tell that she was putting a boundary between them. "This is Ben."

"Nice to meet you," Rafael said, coming around the desk and sticking out his hand. "I was just offering Jessica my congratulations," he clarified. "For a good debate."

Ben eyed him, while they still shook hands. "I'm sure you were."

"Well, I should get out of here," he said. "I've got a late dinner to attend."

Jessica extended her hand. "Well, thank you for a great debate, Councilman. I can't wait to do it again."

* * *

Rafael wished he'd just gone home instead of meeting Alana and the guys. Seated at the best table at Thalia, a restaurant owned by The Brotherhood, his friends gave him worried looks, averting their eyes when he looked back. He was angry, frustrated and horny—each feeling playing for dominance inside him—and he knew he wasn't very good company. While his friends chatted, he didn't take part, and instead spent his time in his own head, wondering how Jessica had gotten the better of him, how she'd so fully gotten under his skin.

"So, are we going to discuss your debate or not?" Gabe asked, cutting into his steak, and finally bringing Rafael into the conversation.

"Nope," Rafael said simply and ate a forkful of his own porterhouse.

"Yeah, what happened, man?" Brett asked. "It was pretty rough to watch."

"I thought it was going well at first, but things got off track toward the end there," he admitted. "Jessica's impassioned, and she's appealing to people's emotions, their fears. And I get it. People are sick of the same no-action politicians. But, man, I didn't think she'd be so formidable an opponent."

"And about Jessica," Alana started carefully. "I saw her at the club last night. Before you escorted her upstairs?" she asked, raising an eyebrow. Shit. He thought when he'd left his friends at the table, they'd been too tipsy to notice who he was meeting. Alana shrugged. "I run the place, not much happens that I don't see."

"I just wanted to talk to her in private," he explained. He ran his tongue over his bottom lip before he reached for his water. But he could still taste her.

Alana lowered her fork and turned to fully face him. "You have two offices, there are dozens of conference rooms in the building," she reminded him. "And at least a dozen more places where you could *talk* that don't contain a bed and a fully stocked minibar."

Gabe's eyes widened expectantly, and Brett and Alex both snorted into their glasses. Rafael knew the other men at the table were glad they weren't the ones under Alana's shrewd attack. When she wanted to know something, there was nothing that could steer her off course.

"What do you want from me?" he asked her. "We had a good time."

"As good of a time as you had in San Francisco last weekend?" Alex asked, his eyebrow raised, looking to stir the pot a little, and make Rafael stew.

The rest of the table looked at him. They hadn't known about his impromptu trip out of state, and he'd hoped to keep it that way, but he knew all his secrets would come out eventually. There weren't any secrets within The Brotherhood.

"When were you in San Francisco?" Brett asked.

Rafael looked at Alex, daring him to say something. His glare wasn't enough, however, because Alex smirked. "He went to see Jessica."

Four sets of eyes turned to him.

"You son of a bitch," Rafael muttered.

"What happened?" Gabe asked. "What was she doing in California?"

"He isn't telling," Alex offered.

"She's your political opponent. Are you guys sleeping together, and what, going on vacations together?" Alana asked. When he didn't respond, she frowned. "You aren't going to share any details?"

Rafael wouldn't kiss and tell, and he'd keep Jessica's secret, but he didn't like withholding things from his friends. "It's complicated. I can't talk about it," he said, knowing that wouldn't do anything to sate his friends' curiosity.

"Rafael Martinez is reluctant to share the details of his sex life?" Brett laughed. "Now we know you're in trouble."

"You don't see it as a problem that you're having sex with your rival?" Alana asked.

"Jesus." Rafael's voice rose, frustrated. He'd hoped only for a relaxing dinner with his friends, but he'd found himself facing the gauntlet. "What is this inquisition? We're not sleeping together. We're just hanging out, getting to know each other, as colleagues." He knew it was a lie. Only an hour ago, he'd kissed her, eaten from her, in her office. He could still taste her on his lips. And he was still hungry for her, and he wouldn't be satisfied until he had her again.

"Next time, why not try being vague?" Brett joked.

He looked around the table at his friends. "You're all assholes, you know that, right?" He pointed at Alana and Alex, who both smiled when he said, "Especially you two." After the snickers quieted, Rafael picked up his water glass and took a sip. Alex's smile had turned to a frown, and Rafael knew he didn't approve of any interaction he might have with Jessica. "Just say it," Rafael said to him.

"I'm just worried that you're losing focus. There's no reason she should have been able to win the debate over you, unless you were off your game." Maybe he was—he'd never failed to express himself to a crowd before tonight. "This might be a diversion to keep your mind off the election. And even if she isn't trying to distract you, whatever you guys have going on can definitely get in the way of the campaign."

"No," Rafael insisted, although his friend spoke the truth. He hadn't expected to lose the debate, and she'd utterly destroyed him on that stage. If his performance continued to be so lackluster, then he would surely lose the election. He shook his head. "Don't worry about this. It won't affect the campaign, or the business. I've got everything under control," he told them, not sure he believed that statement himself. *Famous last words.*

Riding high from her debate success and another spectacular orgasm at the hands and mouth of Rafael Martinez, Jessica had gone for a few rounds of celebratory margaritas with Ben. Several hours later, they stumbled, giggling, into their house, said good-night and went promptly to bed. But even though she was dog-tired and tipsy from the tequila, she was unable to keep her eyes closed. Despite the fact that she hadn't slept much the night before, and despite the fact that she'd ingested more tequila than a human body could possibly handle, sleep completely evaded her, and she rolled over onto her back and stared at the ceiling. The glow of the streetlights and passing cars outside lit her bedroom, casting shadows throughout the room. She watched them, hoping that the gentle lights would help her doze off.

Nope.

Jessica exhaled a frustrated sigh, as the red numbers of her digital clock told her it was after midnight and she'd been in bed for over an hour. It was Rafael's fault that she was still up. Being with him the night before, and that evening in her office, plagued her. Under the blankets, her fingers touched her thighs where he'd held her. Her skin felt hot, as if his fingers had singed into her flesh, leaving stinging wounds. All she could think about was how easily she'd allowed Rafael to take her over. When he got near her, her brain shut off, and her loins were 100 percent in charge. The thought sobered her. No matter what he knew about her, no matter how vulnerable he'd made her, she couldn't help it. He could ruin everything for her, but she just couldn't stop herself around him, and that feeling burned within her. Even now, she could feel herself become damp, wetting the panties she'd worn to bed. She wanted Rafael.

She looked over at her bedside table. Her cell phone was charging. She disconnected it and before she could tell herself not to, she opened Rafael's contact information, typed him a quick Hey and put the phone down.

She only had to wait a few seconds for a response. What are you doing?

I can't sleep.

His response was immediate. Me neither.

How was dinner?

Good. There was a delay. I want to see you again. Tomorrow. Come over to my place, we can have dinner.

Why?

Because I've been thinking about you all night.

Me, too.

What are you doing right now? he asked her.

I'm in bed. You?

Same. Are you naked?

She looked down at her tank top and panties. Yes, she lied.

Why don't you send me a picture?

Jessica smiled. You want a nude?

Yeah. Why not?

You'll keep it to yourself?

Of course I will.

She couldn't. Right? He, along with many others, had already seen her naked. She could hide her face and still give Rafael what he wanted. She giggled and sat up, putting down her phone for a moment. She stripped off her tank top, then turned on the bedside lamp and held her phone above her, her front-facing camera helping her align the device so that she took a photo of her torso from the mouth down. That way if it got out, no one would know it was her.

Before she could think better of it, she hit Send. And added a follow-up message. Your turn.

Rafael gripped his phone, waiting for her next message. He wasn't sure what to expect, a nude or a prompt *go fuck yourself.* That was the thing with Jessica Morgan, she always kept him guessing. After dinner, he'd gone to bed, tried to sleep, but it didn't happen. The book he'd used to distract himself hadn't worked. He was tense, edgy, and from the moment he'd taken his mouth from between Jessica's thighs, he hadn't been able to concentrate on anything but getting back there. No matter how long a cold shower he'd taken, or the number of times he'd taken matters into his own hands, nothing had been able to make his body forget about the way she felt. But thinking about Jessica also led him to think about the man who'd walked in on them in her office. Who was he?

When his phone dinged at the arrival of Jessica's message, he sat up and quickly opened the picture. The sight of her full breasts, trim stomach and her devilish grin about did him in.

He laughed to himself at her text, and replied. I don't think so.

Why not? You want me to trust you, show me why I should.

Jessica had one hell of a point. If he had any shot of currying her favor, seeing her again, she needed to trust him. He smiled, his heartbeat racing, pumping blood southward, and he pushed himself out of bed. Naked, he strode into his closet and stood in front of the full-length mirror. He knew he had a good body. He worked hard on it. Over the last decade, since he'd been voted in to city council, there'd been magazine articles and online posts citing him as the city's, and one of the country's, sexiest politicians and most eligible bachelors. He spent hours in the gym, whenever he wasn't working, to maintain his physique. And it showed. His body tensed as he flexed his muscles slightly, and when he was satisfied with the result, he snapped the picture and sent it to Jessica. Like her, he didn't include his face, but definitely captured his cock, now erect and pointing upward, a result of the picture she'd sent him, which he wouldn't be deleting anytime soon.

He was heading back to his bed when he got her simple response. Nice.

Think it'll get you through the night?

Hopefully.

Why don't you let me come over to your place? I can make you scream once again, and then we might be able to get some sleep. There was another delay before her next message, and he was sure for a moment that she wouldn't respond.

Ben probably wouldn't appreciate the screaming.

Ben, again. Who the fuck was that guy? You may be right. Rafael tried to play it cool. And even though he knew there might be another man in her life, he was only seconds from suggesting she sneak out and come over to his place, but then her message came through.

I'll see you tomorrow.

CHAPTER TEN

RAFAEL DRUMMED HIS fingers on his desk, and he looked at his watch. It was almost five, and for the first time in as long as he could remember, he was leaving the office when everyone else did. He'd finished all his work and he wasn't sticking around. He was anxious to see Jessica, and for the entire day it was all that he could think about. He picked up his phone and for the thousandth time that day, he looked at the topless photo she'd sent him, and each time it stoked the fires within him higher and higher, until his clothing felt tight and constricting. In his entire life, he'd never been so completely captivated by a woman. Normally with a lover, he'd be able to do the deed and move on. But with Jessica, he was incapable.

He looked at his watch as the second hand passed the top, signaling that it was five. "Fuck this," he muttered and stood from his desk. Jessica wouldn't be coming by his house for a couple of hours, but as long as he wasn't getting more work done, he might as well just leave, go to the gym, maybe, see if one of the guys was available for a session. At least try to get rid of some of the excess energy he had.

As he was packing his laptop into his shoulder bag, Jillian bounded into the room, her arms full of stacks of file folders. "Oh." She stopped short in the doorway when she saw him. "You're leaving?"

"Yeah," he said with a shrug. "I work late all the time, I didn't think I needed permission to leave at the day's end." He tried not to sound so defensive, but it didn't work.

"Of course not, I just thought that we could go over the latest polls, and strategize how to overcome Morgan's surge in popularity."

He knew he should agree and stick around. But he was antsy. He needed to get out of the office. He needed to see Jessica. "I can't tonight. I've got a meeting."

She frowned. "There's nothing in your calendar about an evening meeting."

"It just came up last night," he told her. He had to get out of his office. "Let's go over strategy tomorrow, okay?"

"Yeah, sure," Jillian said to his back, as Rafael walked out the door ahead of her. He didn't turn around, but he could feel her eyes on his back as he walked into the elevator.

Rafael popped open the lids from the carryout trays, and laid them out on the dining room table. He could have cooked, his mother would be mortified that he hadn't, but why would he, when he had a Michelin-star chef at

Thalia who could do it for him. Everything looked and
smelled amazing and he realized that he hadn't eaten
since earlier that morning, having worked through lunch
in an effort to be able to leave the office on time. But it
wasn't as though he'd gotten much done. Hell, all he'd
done in the two days since they'd been together was try
to find a way to shake past the need for Jessica. He'd
worked on several projects, barked his way through
a couple of meetings and he'd beaten Brett's ass in a
training session with their personal trainer, an MMA
fighter who coached them weekly. The sessions had always been a good way to work off stress and tension.
But today it had done nothing but leave Brett walking
away with a limp.

But outside every stop, there was at least one reporter waiting to talk to him, to get a sound bite, luring
him into saying something negative about his opponent. But he never took the bait. He'd been in politics
long enough to know better. But in his recent memory,
he couldn't recall a municipal election that had drawn
the curiosity and attention of the people in the way he
and Jessica had.

There was a knock on the door, and he smiled, knowing it was her. He tried to control the speed of his gait
as he walked to the door to greet her. When he pulled
it open, however, it wasn't Jessica that greeted him, it
was Alex. "Hey, what's up?"

"I was in the neighborhood," he said, pushing in.
"Thought I'd pop by."

He narrowed his eyes, knowing that his friend lived

all the way across town. "You never pop by. You're very much against the *pop by*. What's up?"

"I just wanted to check on you. You really went hard in training today. I was just wondering with the campaign ramping up and the election getting closer, and whatever the hell you've got going on with Jessica, if you're doing okay."

"I appreciate your concern, but everything is fine. It's a stressful time. And I'm sorry if Brett couldn't handle our session, but at least now he's back at home, with Rebecca playing nursemaid. Maybe he got soft while he was away on his honeymoon. But I'm okay."

"Dude, I'm not fucking around here. You need to tell me what happened in San Francisco. You went there to catch her stripping and use it against her campaign. But you haven't told me what's up. You haven't done anything to throw off her campaign. Now you guys are spending all this time together. Man, talk to me."

"Nothing's going on," Rafael said immediately. He hated lying to his friend—he'd never done it before. He and Alex had known each other since they were children, and seen each other through thick and thin. "This thing with Jessica, I don't know what's going on, but—"

A knock at the door stopped his words. His head whipped around to the sound, and he turned back to face Alex, who just seemed to take in the bottle of wine, open on the counter, two glasses poured, the set table and the two take-out containers that held food.

"You expecting someone?"

"Yes, and it wasn't you." Rafael opened the door

to find Jessica. She smiled when she saw him, but she frowned when she looked over his shoulder, seeing Alex standing next to the table.

"Don't mind him," he told her. "He was just leaving." He turned to his friend. "I'll see you tomorrow."

"Yeah, you will," Alex muttered and walked out the door, leaving him and Jessica alone.

"What was that about?" she asked.

"Nothing," Rafael said, handing her a glass of wine. "Why don't you take a seat. Dinner's ready."

She looked at the plastic carryout trays. "I thought you were cooking."

"I was going to. But then I realized that I haven't picked up groceries since the campaign started, and even if I did, I wouldn't have time to cook anyway. I mean, I could have cooked this. But instead, I found a chef to do the work."

She laughed. The sound was pleasant in his ears. "Well, it certainly looks good."

"I stopped at Thalia on my way home."

"Oh, nice, Ben took me out there for my birthday last year."

"Ben," he repeated, a hint of annoyance in his voice. He didn't know who the man was, but he already didn't like him.

"Yeah, the guy who stopped by my office after the debate last night, after we—" She stopped and narrowed her eyes at him. "Are you jealous of Ben?" she asked, with a laugh.

His laugh was short. "No, I'm not jealous." He was

always so sure and secure. He rarely wasted any time on jealousy.

She sauntered closer, as he busied himself pouring them some wine. "Ben lives with me. Are you sure you aren't jealous?"

"Nope." He played it cool. If she was involved with Ben, then everything that they'd done together would mean she was a cheater. And he thought less about cheaters than most. "Jealousy isn't really my thing."

"I love Ben," she whispered, a smart smirk turning her red lips upward. "He's the last person I see before I go to bed, and the first I see in the morning…"

"And what's he doing tonight, seeing as how you're here with me? And what about when you go to San Francisco? Where is he then?"

"I think tonight he's out on a date with a gorgeous but incredibly stupid fireman."

Rafael smiled, realization dawning on him. "He's gay."

"He is," she confirmed, taking her wineglass. "And you're jealous."

He clinked his glass against hers. "I'm not jealous."

"Sure," she said, clearly not believing him, as she sipped and turned away from him. "This is a pretty nice place."

"Thanks, but I can't take credit. My friend Alana designed it, decorated it and ordered all the furniture. I wish I had the opportunity to spend a little more time here, though."

"You spend a lot of your nights at your room at Di

Terrestres, I know. So, why are you running for mayor? It will only take up more time."

He didn't answer her, and instead plated their meals and brought them over to the table. "Chicken tetrazzini or turkey Bolognese?"

"Chicken, please."

He set the food in front of her and handed her cutlery and a napkin. "I want to be mayor because a career in politics has always been my dream. First the city, then the senate, then the White House."

"Lofty goals," she said. "The people of Las Vegas are just your stepping-stone to the rest of the country?"

He sighed heavily. "You always say things like that. Like I'm just here doing all this work for my own personal gain. But that's not the case. I have money, yes, I don't need politics. But because I'm in such a position, I want to do what I can, when I can, to help people. I can make this city better, I know it. But bigger and better will always be my goal, no matter which heights I reach." He looked over at her.

"There's more, though, isn't there? What about personally? You maintain that I don't know who you are, so tell me."

"Well, you know my family immigrated here. My mom and dad both worked hard. Dad got a job in a casino as a janitor, and Mom worked part-time at our school. They made sure to instill the value of hard work in us. They made sure we stayed in school, excelled, went to college. But it wasn't a free ride. I got some scholarships, but otherwise, I paid for it myself. It still amounted to quite a bit of student loan debt. I struggled for years, and I pulled myself out of it. That doesn't make me a bad person, and it doesn't mean I've forgotten where I come from."

"Where are your parents now?"

"They're still here. They have a home in Henderson."

"And your sisters?"

"Three sisters." He smiled. "Two older, one younger. They're a pain, but I love them. They also live here, but my youngest sister is in Haiti right now, working with a humanitarian project down there."

"If you come from such humble beginnings, how did you get into business? Even though you keep them quiet, you've got some pretty good connections." She took an appraising look around his home. "You've obviously been successful."

He nodded. "I have been. Being a Las Vegas city councillor isn't what made me rich, but it's the work that's close to my heart. I made the right investments, trusted the right people. But it's been a group effort. Alex, Brett, Alana, Gabe, we all work together on our ventures. We each do our part and bring something to the table. The money we make gets invested back into the rest of the businesses. The Brotherhood's built itself quite a comfortable little empire," he finished with a smile.

"And political clout, that's what you bring to the table, isn't it?"

He shrugged and smirked, but didn't respond. He'd be lying if he said he'd never used his name, or position, in the city to make life easier for his friends. There were all sorts of people he was interested in helping, including the business community. Maybe it muddied the waters a bit, but if it got things done—made positive change in the long run—then he didn't mind. "I think that's enough about me. What about you? What's your story?"

Jessica played with the stem of her glass, looking into the dark red liquid, as she turned the glass in circles. "Well, I'm from here. Born and raised in Las Vegas. My mother was a showgirl, like with the feathers and dancing and all that. I didn't know my father, he left before I was born." She ran a finger along the lip of her glass. "Even though I was left alone a lot—Mom worked nights, obviously—she always made up for it. I never lacked for love or attention."

He sipped his wine. "When did you start stripping?"

"I started *dancing* in college," she corrected him. "I needed a job I could do on the weekends, but like you, I also needed help paying my tuition and bills. From growing up with my mom, I'd learned some tricks that look good onstage, plus I took some lessons when we could afford it." She smiled faintly. "But I was so nervous on my first night. They just kind of threw me onstage. So, I basically winged it and shook my ass and did a few tricks for a three-minute song, and I made four hundred dollars that night." She shrugged. "But as it turns out I was really good at it. I got better, I trained with dance instructors, learned how to pole dance and honed my craft, all while I studied and completed a political science degree. But when I graduated, instead of looking for a regular day job, I kept dancing. Then I started getting more attention, and took part in competitions. Started winning. I've actually won international championships for pole dancing."

"Really?" He was impressed. "And now you're giving it all up for a run at the mayor's office?"

She nodded, taking her first bite of chicken. "Like a lot of people in this city, I'm tired of the status quo and feeling underrepresented by those in power. I knew there needed to be a change. And I figured as long as there were only rich men in power, I knew that change wouldn't come about."

"And your message is resonating with the people."

"It seems to be. There's a lot of frustration, locally and throughout the country."

"You know, you really are doing a great job. For someone who's as new as you are, to come in and make such a big splash, it's surprising. You're making me work a hell of a lot harder than I thought I would." He was sincere in his compliments. Her success was commendable.

She looked up from her food. "Thank you."

"So, do you have any plans this weekend?"

"I'm going to San Francisco," she told him.

The news wasn't pleasant for him, and he frowned but said nothing. He brought some pasta to his mouth, and chewed. It was delicious, but he barely tasted it. He didn't have a claim to her, but he didn't like the idea of her onstage, in front of strangers.

He looked up at her, and saw that she was looking at him, frowning. "What?" she asked, obviously able to see through his silence.

"I didn't know that you would still be dancing. I thought you were done, once I saw you there."

"I've decided to go back one last time before the election. Hopefully that'll get it out of my system."

"I don't like it," he said, simply. He didn't mean to say it, it just slipped out.

She looked taken aback. "Well, that's not for you to decide. Plus, my campaign can always use more money."

"The Kickstarter hasn't raised enough?"

She glared at him across the table. "You're an asshole. Why should political office only be for the people who can afford to run a campaign? Representation for everyone matters."

"It does. I'm in full agreement with you. But I guess I just don't understand why you still strip, even though you've been with the council for a couple of years, making a decent salary. It's so exploitative."

She leaned in, her gaze hard and unwavering. "Rafael, I'll let you in on a secret. Politics is far more exploitative than anything I've ever done on the stage. As a dancer, no one hounds me in the streets or clamors to know about my personal life. But for whatever reason, this election has made people want to know about us. I'm actually surprised it hasn't come out yet. But when I'm onstage, I'm free. It's fun. People are there to see me, and they don't expect anything more from me than simple entertainment."

He nodded. Maybe she had a point. He forked some more pasta into his mouth, and chewed thoughtfully.

"And now you're pouting."

"I'm not pouting."

"Ha!" she snickered. "Be more of a jealous man, why don't you?"

He laughed bitterly, as well. He'd never been the jealous type, but Jessica seemed to bring it out in him.

"Why does it matter to you what I do on the weekends? You say you aren't jealous, but why do you care? You aren't even supposed to like me, remember? But yet, you don't like the idea of other men seeing me? So, what is it?" she asked.

"You know what? It doesn't matter," he said, bringing their plates to the kitchen. He washed his hands, and from its space in a nearby cupboard, he withdrew the black-and-gold envelope that he'd been looking forward to giving her. "But I have something for you. There's a party at Di Terrestres next Saturday. It's our yearly masquerade for our members. Everyone dresses up, we wear masks. It's a lot of fun. I want you to come." He'd never brought a date to the party before. He'd never asked Jessica out on a date.

She accepted it and fingered the flap. "I don't know. What if people see us together?"

"That again? Like I told you. It's safe there. You'll be wearing a mask, and if anyone did see you, they couldn't say anything anyway."

"But the press…"

"Aren't allowed in. Decide later," he told her, "but for now, come on." He picked up the bottle. "Want some more wine?"

"Sure. Where are we going?"

"It's a nice night. Let's go outside," he said. He grabbed the bottle and crossed the floor to the doors that led to his balcony, where he'd already set everything up.

The hot tub bubbled. Both it and the pool were lit from the bottom and looked inviting in the cool night air. The notes of Mexican guitar surrounded them, his favorite music. A throwback to his roots. It was sexy, mellow, and it relaxed him. He hoped she felt the same.

"Wow," she said, looking visibly impressed. "This is how the 1 percenters live, hey?"

He ignored the gibe and turned to her. "Want to go for a swim?"

"It's a bit chilly."

"I'll keep you warm."

"I forgot my bathing suit."

"What, are you afraid to get naked?" he challenged, putting down the wine bottle and then kicking off his shoes. "Sounds like you're just trying to find excuses."

When he looked up at her, she was already in the process of pulling her shirt over her head. "Never."

He stopped in place and smiled at her willingness to strip to her bra and panties. When she reached back to unclasp her bra, she paused and looked at him. "What's the holdup? Are *you* afraid to get naked?" she challenged him.

"The picture that I sent you last night should tell you otherwise," he told her, while unbuttoning his shirt. He shucked his shirt and dipped his fingers under the waistband of his pants and boxers, dropping them to his ankles.

The way her eyes roamed up and down his now naked body gave him a surge of satisfaction. "Your turn," he said, waiting for her to get rid of her bra and underwear.

She followed suit, and he took in her naked body. She was perfect—all smooth, soft skin, curvaceous, and he could see the firm muscle that came about from her time on the stage. Naked, he stalked toward her, a predatory growl that started low in his belly made its way upward and passed through his parted lips as he reached her.

He wrapped his arms around her waist and pulled her to him. She went to him willingly, his upright cock pressing into her stomach, which was warm against him. Rafael wanted to bury himself deep inside of her. But first, he gripped her tightly, and jumped into the pool, pulling her in with him. When they surfaced, she laughed and punched him in the shoulder. "Jerk," she said with a smile, pushing her wet hair, the golden brown made dark by the water, behind her shoulders. "Why did you do that?" she asked, before swimming away.

"I don't know." He laughed again and followed her

to the edge of the pool where he'd placed their wine. "I just felt like it, I guess. I felt hot. So did you."

It felt good to just laugh with her. They'd spent so much time arguing, being contentious in the media, and during council meetings, but he was quickly learning that not only was she stubborn and frustrating, and sexy beyond his wildest fantasies, but she was also a lot of fun to be around.

Jessica shivered. Rafael's body was warm, but the cool, late October air was chilly.

"Cold?" he asked, pulling her more fully against him. Her palms flattened against his chest and then she fisted the dark curly hair that covered it.

"A little."

"Want to move to the hot tub?"

She nodded, and he brought them to the pool's edge where he lifted her out, so she sat on the concrete. She watched every muscle in his upper body work as he pushed himself out, and her mouth dropped. He was a powerful, devastatingly sexy man; his body was perfect.

Jessica settled into the hot tub, and let her body still as the jets of water hit her fatigued muscles. She sighed deeply. She heard him slip into the water beside her. And he passed over her wineglass. She took it and watched him. He was quiet, but she could tell there was something on his mind.

"What's up? You look like you're a million miles away."

He laughed. "Do you like me yet?" he asked with a lopsided grin.

Despite herself, she smiled and shrugged. Something was definitely forming between them. Whether it was a newfound respect for him, or just physical, she had to admit that her long-held opinions of him were beginning to change. "I think I'm getting there," she admitted.

"I'd like to go to San Francisco with you."

She shook her head. "No."

"Why not?"

"I've seen what happens when guys come to watch their girlfriends dance. They always claim to be cool with it, and then they get all crazy and possessive. It always ends terribly."

"Well, you're not my girlfriend," he offered, needlessly. "And I'd like to see you dance again."

"I know, but you were about frothing at the mouth over Ben. I can't imagine you at a club."

"I've seen you dance before."

"Things are different now." She didn't know exactly how it had happened but since the night they'd met in San Francisco, he'd started to wear down her resolve. She *was* starting to like him. A lot. And even though they were still competitors, rivals, they were able to sit together, naked in a hot tub, joking and laughing, a prelude to the amazing sex they would soon have.

"All right. I won't go," he said. It surprised her to hear him concede. "But you can take the jet."

The jet? "No, I'm fine. I've got my tickets booked already. I can pay my own way." She didn't need his help. It wasn't about the money.

"It's not about that. But this could be your opportunity to fly on your own schedule." He smirked. "You know, you might be the only person to fight me on the offer of a private jet."

"I'm just not used to having people help me like that. I grew up relying on myself. I never imagined that you'd be the guy offering me help."

"Maybe you should learn to accept some help, every now and then. There's nothing wrong with it—wasn't that your point at the debate?"

His words surprised her. She didn't have trouble accepting help from others, did she? She shrugged and turned back to her wineglass. Still, taking the favor of a private jet ride wasn't what she'd meant. Without answering him, she leaned back and closed her eyes, letting the powerful jets of the hot tub pulse against her muscles. Her body was completely relaxed, but her mind was racing. His home, his life, was comfortable and luxurious, and while dancing helped her financially— she'd been able to buy a nicer house than she could have imagined, she could afford to travel and allow herself small luxuries like the six-dollar coffee she needed every morning—her lifestyle was still fairly modest, in comparison. She sneaked a peek at Rafael. He had given up on getting a response, and he was also leaning back, enjoying the spoils of his opulent life, as if it was nothing.

With a frown, she realized that she didn't fit into his life at all. Discussing private jet usage, in a hot tub on the patio of a luxury home, sipping expensive wine, this wasn't her. She grew restless. And she put down her glass and shifted to get out of the tub. He reached out and grasped her wrist before she could fully stand.

"Where are you going?" he asked.

"I've got to get home."

"Already?"

"Rafael, just let me go."

He did. "Why don't you tell me what's making you want to leave so quickly. I thought we were having a good time."

"I need to leave. I have a life, work to do."

"Nothing else?"

Jessica sighed. "I don't know what we're doing here, Rafael. Look at us. We shouldn't be doing this. We're opponents, you're—" she waved a hand "—you're *all this*. And I'm not."

"So that means we can't hang out? Drink wine and have great sex?"

She looked around again, trying to remind herself why she couldn't spend time with him. "But we're so different," she said, her voice low and her constitution weak.

"We're still people. We might be competitors, but you'll notice that the things we have in common are growing by the day. We both love our families, we both want to help people, we're extremely sexually compatible. Why not just let it happen? And see where we go?"

"But where are we going?"

He stood and extended his hand to her. She watched

as the rivulets of water trailed over his smooth dark skin. "Right now, I'm not interested in that, I'm more interested in where we are right now."

Rafael tugged her wrist until she sat again. He passed her her wineglass, and they drank in companionable silence. She twisted her hair on top of her head, somehow managing to knot it in place, with only a few wet tendrils snaking around her shoulders. He reached out and pinched one and then wrapped it around his finger. The humor in both of their smiles faded, and he saw the moment when her eyes heated with desire.

"This is crazy," she whispered.

"I know."

He put his arms around her, pulling her to him, and kissed her. She tasted like wine, but her own taste was just as intoxicating. His tongue searched her mouth, licking, tasting, drinking her in. Her moans, as his hands traveled down her bare back, vibrated from her throat to his, and they made him keep going, wanting to explore more. He lifted her, and in the water, she was almost weightless in his arms. Her lean, muscled thighs wrapped tightly around his waist.

His mouth kissed its way from her lips, over her jaw, then down the fine line of her throat, and over her shoulder, before he raised her higher and laved attention over her full, high breasts. He took a rosy, peaked nipple into his mouth, and in response she clutched his head and pulled him closer. With his face pressed into her chest, he couldn't breathe. He could suffocate in her breasts. *But what a way to go.*

His dick was pressing upward against the lower part of her ass, and he pushed his hips up so it slid against her. In response to him, she moaned and held him tighter between her legs. He lifted her so she was sitting on the edge of the tub, and he followed her, pushing himself up and out until he laid on top of her. He kissed her again, parting her knees with his own. He notched his dick at her opening, and he somehow managed to stop himself before pushing inside of her, when he remembered the condom he'd left in his pants. Luckily, they were nearby and within reach. He pulled it from his pocket and quickly rolled the latex over his length.

Kneeling, he was inspired. He turned her so that she was on her stomach and then pulled her hips to meet him, and he slid home. Her sigh was jagged and breathy as she pushed back against him. He pumped his hips forward and back, meeting her, burying himself deeply inside of her. One hand snaked around to her front and found her clit. He circled two fingers over her and he dropped his hand on her ass with a heavy smack that made her cry out. She looked over her shoulder at him, and her eyes flashed in desire.

"Oh, God," she whispered, her breath reduced to heavy gasps. And with just a couple of thrusts, he felt her clench and tighten around his dick. Spasming in pleasure. He came with a shout, allowing her muscles to milk him until he'd filled the condom. He broke away from her and took a second to dispose of it, and she took the opportunity to settle back into the hot tub. Her eyes were hooded, and her smile was satisfied. The picture of beauty, and he joined her and pulled her close. She shivered in his arms.

"Still cold?"

She nodded. "A little."

The air was cool on their wet, heated skin, so he scooped her up in his arms, and carried her inside to his bedroom.

CHAPTER ELEVEN

THE PEAL OF Rafael's cell phone woke him the next morning. When he opened his eyes, two things were apparent to him. First, he was well rested after a suspicious amount of sleep, and the sun was higher in the sky than it normally was at six in the morning, his usual waking time. And, second, when he rolled over to find his phone, he remembered that he wasn't alone.

He looked to the other side of his bed and remembered that Jessica was next to him and had been all night. She was waking, as well, and she sleepily looked up at him as he reached over her for his phone. "This is Martinez," he answered.

"Hey, Rafael, it's Jillian. I just wanted to make sure you were okay. It being nine, after all, and you aren't here yet."

9:00 a.m.? Shit. He'd slept past nine. He hadn't slept that late since he'd been a child. It had been a long time since he'd spent a night with a woman like Jessica. They'd stayed up for hours, talking. And when they hadn't been doing that, they'd used their mouths for other purposes, until, spent, they'd both collapsed into the bed and slept, fully wrapped up in one another.

"Yeah, everything's fine. I just got a bit of a late start to my day. I'm actually working from my home office this morning. So, if you could forward any calls to my cell phone, I'd really appreciate it. I'll be in later this afternoon."

"Yeah, sure. If you need anything else, just let me know."

"Will do." He hung up, and turned to Jessica.

"What time is it?" she asked.

"Ten past nine."

"Oh, God," she muttered.

"So, you don't normally sleep in this late, either?"

"I don't, and I haven't in years," she said, pushing herself out of bed. Rafael's eyes locked on the smooth skin of her back and her ass. He almost groaned with need. "Mind if I use your shower?"

"Go right ahead."

She paused and pursed her lips. "Want to join me?"

Rafael's mouth opened, about to say yes. But his cell phone rang in his hand. He looked at it and saw it was city council business. He had to take it. But that didn't mean that every fiber of his body wasn't trying to make him go into the bathroom with her. But his brain won out. "I can't. I have work to do. I'm already behind."

Jessica stepped out of the shower and realized the clothes she'd worn the night before were probably still poolside, so, wrapped in a fluffy towel, she found one of Rafael's dress shirts slung over a chair and pulled it on. It smelled like him—spicy, leathery, but with a hint of sweetness—just like him. She pulled the collar and inhaled.

She walked to the kitchen. Rafael was sitting at his kitchen table dressed in only a pair of gray sweatpants, sipping coffee and reading on a tablet. He didn't notice as she came up behind him, marveling in the broad expanse of his back. He was gorgeous, powerful, all hard muscle under dark skin. He turned his head and saw her walk toward him.

He gestured with the tablet. "Looks like I'm ahead again," he informed her.

"Is that so?" she asked, heading for the coffee maker. He'd taken a mug out for her, so she poured herself a coffee and joined him at the table. Looking over his shoulder, she read the article. It was true, Rafael was up, and she was down. Again. They'd traded leads every day. They'd been neck and neck for a week now. To hide her worry, she pointed to the picture above the article, one of him at a city gala, wearing a tuxedo and a bright smile that formed dimples on each of his cheeks. "That's a really sexy picture of you. I'll bet that's why you're ahead, people want to vote for you because you're pretty."

"Is that right?" he asked with an amused smile.

She nodded. "This is definitely the year of the good-looking politicians. You're on trend."

He looked at her, silent for a minute before he threw his head back with laughter. "Your logic is a little flawed, if we're talking about good-looking candidates," he told her, looking her up and down. He put down the tablet and turned to her. They sipped their coffees in silence, watching one another over the rims of their coffee mugs. It was such a comfortable, domestic thing—just two lovers enjoying their morning coffee before they tackled their days.

The ring of her own cell phone sent her head on a swivel, trying to locate where she'd dropped her purse the night before. She finally found it in the foyer. It was Gordon.

"Jessica, have you seen the latest numbers?"

"Yeah, I just did."

"I've got a full day, but we should get together this evening. We should reexamine our strategy. If anyone can capitalize on this type of upswing, it's Martinez."

Gordon was right, and she conceded. "All right. I've got some meetings this afternoon, but let's get together with the team later." She disconnected the call, and turned to Rafael. "I've got to leave."

"Will I see you again tonight?"

"Hmm, maybe," she purred, easily falling back into the role of the smitten lover. She did want to see him again, and was quickly becoming addicted. "I'm meeting with my team tonight," she told him. "Maybe I'll stop by after if it isn't too late."

His hands ran down her back and they cupped her ass. "An emergency meeting to figure out how to beat me?"

"Now you're up in the polls and you're feeling cocky?"

He pushed his hips against her. She could feel his rock-hard cock against her stomach. "You can see how cocky I'm feeling," he said.

She rubbed against him, eliciting a rough groan from him. He tried to hold her closer but she escaped his grip, with a giggle. "I'll see you later."

"Have you thought about the party?"

She could feel the weight of the invitation in her purse. "Yeah, I have. I'll go." He smiled and reached for her, and she allowed herself to be pulled into his arms.

"I'm glad." He kissed her, and it was sweet, unlike many of their bruising kisses, but it was no more devoid of the passion between them. She wrapped her arms around him and allowed it. She was almost fully under his spell when a ringing phone interrupted them. It was his, and they parted.

"You might want to get to work yourself, I'd hate for someone to think you're fooling around when you should be working hard for your constituents."

A couple of hours later, Rafael was in his office at city hall when there was a knock on the door. Usually, Jillian worked out of his other office, and he normally handled his tasks with the city on his own, unless he requested she come here or he needed her to work remotely.

"Come in," he called out. He liked to be accessible to his colleagues and constituents, but he didn't really have the time to be interrupted. He'd fallen behind in his work and he had to play some serious catch-up. The door opened. He was surprised to see Alex. They didn't knock on each other's doors, and instead just walked on in. Rafael rolled his eyes, not interested in talking. He turned back to his computer, and the budget spreadsheets in front of him. "What now?"

"We have to talk." Alex strode in and closed the door behind him.

"If it's the same reason you stopped by last night, I'm not interested."

"Look, I know I'm riding you on this, and I know you're with Jessica, or whatever is going on there. But I'm worried about you."

"You don't need to worry about me. I've got everything under control."

"But I'm not just worried about you. We're all counting on you to win here. The Brotherhood needs this. We don't want to screw this up."

Rafael knew that his rise in politics would shine favorably on the group, but it finally occurred to him that they were all counting on him to succeed, and every minute he lost focus on the race, it meant that he was one point closer to losing. They weren't corrupt, and they wouldn't abuse power, but they would accept any help that came from Rafael being a political leader.

"We at least deserve to know what's going on," Alex implored him, referring to the group of them. "We don't keep secrets."

Rafael shook his head. "No, I can't. The fact that

you know what she does is too much. Everything else is between me and her."

"And what about us? Everything is riding on this."

Rafael didn't speak for a moment. He felt bad. He knew he was screwing up. "You're right. I have lost some of my focus on the mayoral race. But I know how important this is to all of us. I haven't forgotten."

"You're in possession of information that will hand you a solid victory," Alex reminded him. "Can we finally use it?"

"No," Rafael said adamantly.

"What about the fact that she knows about the club? What if she leaks it?"

"She won't."

"We need to get her out of the race, Raf, it's getting down to the wire. You guys are neck and neck. You could lose this."

"I'm not going to win like that, betraying her."

"Well, we need a new plan." Alex stood. "I've got to go, I've got meetings. But think about what I said."

When Rafael was alone again, he sat back in his chair. He knew Alex was right, but he hadn't quite grasped the scope of the importance of his run on his friends. They had plans, and having a contact in the mayor's office would certainly move things along easily for them. Using his position in such a way might sound sketchy to some, but it was the way things got done in his circle.

He needed a victory. But he wasn't willing to betray Jessica to get it. Yet it *was* tempting, to ensure he'd reach his dreams. It would only take one anonymous phone call or email. His eyes slid to his computer, his open in-box. He could email Tanya Roberts from LVTV, or an online gossip rag. But he stopped himself. He wouldn't do it. He couldn't. He threw his head back in the chair and spun away from the desk. He turned to see out the window, looking out at downtown Las Vegas, as people hustled about. As a man who had always held such a tight, firm grasp on his life, how had he entirely let it get fucked-up beyond all reason?

"You didn't come home last night," Ben pointed out, punctuating the sentence with a forkful of kale, pointed at Jessica.

"Don't point your salad at me," she said, smiling. They'd met for lunch at a trendy downtown bistro. She wanted to spend some time with her friend before she got to work that day, and with how busy the next couple of weeks would be for her, she wanted to get in some quality Ben time.

"Where were you? Were you with Rafael again?" When she didn't answer, he went on, talking to himself. "She must have been with Mr. Tall-Dark-and-Handsome, because if there was another guy, she would definitely tell you, Ben, as her favorite person in the universe."

She looked around the restaurant and made sure that there was nobody within listening distance. "Okay, yes, I was with Rafael."

"You are going to have to start sharing some details, honey."

"I don't know what to say."

"Length? Girth?"

"More than adequate. Thanks." She heard someone say her name, and she looked around and saw two young women sitting at a nearby table looking at her. She waved, and the two women got up and approached her at the table. "Ms. Morgan?" one of them asked.

"Yeah, hi. How's it going?"

The girls looked shy, awestruck. "Sorry, we were talking about you. But I just wanted to come over and say what an inspiration you are. You're kicking ass."

"Well, thanks so much."

"No, thank you," the other said. "You're standing up for all of us. You're the voice of every woman who's ever been told to sit down, or let the men handle things. We've actually started an initiative on campus to get people interested in municipal politics and to get out and vote."

Jessica was stunned. "Ladies, thank you so much. You guys are the reason I'm doing this. Your words mean so much to me."

They both looked embarrassed. "Well, we'll just let you get back to your lunch. We just wanted to say thank you."

Jessica could have cried as she watched the young women walk back to their own table. But Ben seemed unfazed and brought the conversation back to sex.

"Unusual kinks?"

Jessica could barely tear her gaze away from the young women. "Outside of the fact that we should be enemies? That we shouldn't even like each other at all? That we're running against each other. That every time we're together, there's an undercurrent of tension. Like we completely forget that it's wrong."

He grinned. "Maybe that's what makes it so fun."

"Yeah, but he's everything that I'm rallying against. And God, his home. He has everything, and it struck me last night how much that isn't my world. And did you see those girls? They believe in me, and look at me, having sex with the one guy I shouldn't be."

"Why do you have to think so much? It's just sex, right?" Ben asked, and then he leaned across the table and peered at her through crinkled eyes. "Unless you *like* him."

Jessica sat back. She did like him. She didn't want to. "I don't know. I shouldn't. He's everything I'm against…or so I thought, because it feels like the more I get to know him, the more I like him." She lifted a forkful of salad to her mouth and chewed thoughtfully. She hadn't allowed herself to think too much about it, but it was true. She got that same nervous flutter when she thought about him, or knew when she was about to see him.

Ben shrugged. "So, you like the guy. What's wrong with that?"

"It's not like we can have anything between us," she said, shaking her head. "I couldn't be with a man like that. Sure, we're sexually compatible, but you certainly can't build a relationship from only that. We're too different. He's everything I'm fighting against, he's arrogant, smug, argumentative, demanding. I can't be with a man like that."

"Are you trying to convince me, or yourself?"

Jessica frowned. It felt like Ben knew her better than she knew herself.

"Are you going to see him again?"

"Yeah," she sighed. "He invited me to the masquerade party at Di Terrestres next weekend."

"So, you don't like him, but you're going to continue to see him."

"It's fucked, I know."

"Are you sure you aren't just trying to find excuses to not be happy. Are you afraid to let him get too close, because if you do, you might learn that he in fact isn't just another spoiled rich guy?"

Jessica watched her friend, but she said nothing. Ben was perceptive, and hearing him say the words out loud made her think. Perhaps she did like Rafael more than she wanted to. She'd spent too long thinking of him as the enemy. The man that represented the root of inequality. And she liked him. What did that say about her?

CHAPTER TWELVE

ON THE NIGHT of the masquerade, Rafael stepped from the back of his car, straightened his tuxedo jacket and fixed his black mask over his eyes. The masquerade party was one of Di Terrestres's most popular events, and it was one of his own favorites, but he felt a nervous twitch in his stomach. That happened more and more when he thought about seeing Jessica. He had offered to pick her up in his own car, but Jessica told him she would rather arrive separately. He knew why. She was becoming increasingly paranoid of being discovered together. He understood it, but he didn't have to like it. So, he'd sent another car for her, and he knew that she'd just arrived before him.

When Rafael entered Di Terrestres, the party was already in full swing. The place was filling up, as most members were eager to attend the twice-yearly party. But as if she had a beacon on her, he instinctively turned his head in her direction and was able to identify her, even though she was wearing a black lace mask that covered the top portion of her face. But even if he hadn't been able to see her face, he would have known her body anywhere.

"That's some dress," he whispered in her ear, seeming to startle her. His eyes raked over her. The dress in question was backless, the V in front plunged almost to her belly button, and the hemline hit the floor, but the slit rose high on her thigh.

She smiled. He could see her green eyes turn mischievous underneath her mask. "I'm glad you like it."

"I more than like it. In fact, I'm going to like it even more when it's balled up on my bedroom floor in a few hours." He leaned down and brushed his lips against hers. He felt her still against him before pulling back.

"Raf," she chided him, looking at the people around them. "I don't know if this is such a good idea."

"I told you, no one cares who we are here."

"I'm sorry, but I don't put so much trust in my fellow man, and NDAs, as you do."

"Just relax," he soothed her, trailing his fingertips down her spine. He felt her responsive, full-body shiver, and he smiled in the knowledge that he could affect her so. "Want to go sit down?"

"Yeah, sure."

A seat was definitely something she needed. That, and a good stiff drink. Even though she tried to keep a steady head, every time she was around Rafael, he clouded her senses and took over her common sense. Going to the party had definitely been a mistake. She couldn't be seen with him in public. It would cripple her campaign if their relationship—*if that's what it is*—got out. Any questions that people had would lead to further digging into her personal life, and then her stripping would be discovered.

Rafael took her hand and led her up a small staircase to a table that overlooked the club. A table that, as she noticed, wasn't empty. Five other people were already seated. One face she immediately recognized—Alex, Rafael's campaign manager, and he frowned at her but quickly covered it. She didn't miss the challenging looks exchanged between Rafael and Alex, who clearly disapproved of her presence. The others she didn't recognize, but from the way they watched her, they all seemed extremely interested in her.

"Everyone, this is Jessica. I invited her to join us tonight." Rafael went around the table and introduced each of his friends, the members of the infamous Brotherhood.

"That explains the extra chair," Brett said.

A stunning blonde woman, Alana, eyed her from across the table. "Well, when Rafael said he was bringing a guest, we weren't really sure what to expect. We certainly didn't expect Jessica Morgan."

The man next to her, Gabe, slung an easy arm over the back of Alana's chair. "Oh, I don't know. I think this is what we all expected."

"Guys," Rafael said to his friends. "Don't be dicks."

"We aren't," Gabe insisted.

"We're being perfectly cordial," Alana agreed, and reached across the table to Jessica. "It's nice to meet you."

"Likewise," Jessica said, shaking her hand. "Thank you all so much for having me." She turned to Rafael. "Thank you for the invite."

"But I'm curious why you're here, though," Alex said.

"Dude," Rafael said, his voice a loud whisper, through what she could tell were clenched teeth.

"It just seems strange to me that you're both spending so much time together, while you're campaigning against one another."

Jessica opened her mouth to respond, but Rafael cut her off, pointing at his friend. "Let's step away from the table, shall we?"

"I'm comfortable right here," Alex responded, settling back in his chair, sipping dark liquid from his glass.

Jessica watched as a silent battle of wills took place between the two men. But she also didn't miss the silent communication between the others at the table— a nonverbal conversation between a close-knit group of friends. After several tense moments, both Rafael and Alex stood.

"We'll be back soon," Rafael told her before they walked away.

Alone in the awkward silence of the table, Jessica frowned. "You know what? I think I'm going to go home. I shouldn't have come."

Again, Alana reached across the table to her. "Oh, don't be silly. Those two have been friends since childhood. They're always fighting about something. They just need to get it out now and then."

"I'm sorry if I caused any trouble for you guys or Rafael."

Brett waved her off. "This isn't exactly a usual situation, you guys being competitors, but don't worry about them. They'll be fine." He sipped his drink. "But this is all very interesting because you're giving Raf a bit of a hard time in the press. I didn't know he was such a masochist."

"I think we can all agree that Rafael could use a hard time every now and then," Jessica said. "Just so he doesn't get soft."

Alana watched her for a moment before she burst into giggles. "Oh, you are good," she said, and then turned to the group. "I like her. Raf better not screw it up."

Jessica felt her cheeks color at Alana's implication. "It's not—" Thankfully, a waitress came by and took their drink order, so she didn't have to address the nature of whatever their relationship was.

Rebecca, Brett's wife, leaned in to her. "How's the campaign going?"

"Really well, thanks," she responded. "It's a lot of work. And I know being mayor will be a much different job than city councillor, but I'm not afraid of a challenge."

"And being so visible in the public eye? You and Raf have your faces splashed everywhere now. That must be difficult."

"I don't mind it so much, I'm just trying to get my

message out there. I'm actually really grateful for all of the free publicity I can get. As long as the story is on my message, and not my personal life, I don't see the problem."

"Are you worried about something in your personal life being exposed?" Gabe asked. She'd been told he was a lawyer, and she could tell by the way he'd honed in on a phrase she hadn't meant to use.

"Aren't we all?" She tried to laugh it off. Gabe didn't seem convinced. "You know what, it's not like I'm embarrassed by it. I'm tired of hiding it." She knew that even though they were Rafael's friends, or maybe *because* they were his friends, the table at Di Terrestres was a safe space for her. If Rafael trusted his friends enough to bring her there, she could probably trust them, as well. She hoped she could. She shrugged. "I'm a stripper." Every pair of eyes at the table turned to her, and she nodded. "Yeah, I'm a dancer. I work in San Francisco most weekends." The group was seemingly stunned into silence, and she continued on. "I've actually won world championships for pole dancing."

It took several more moments before anyone moved and Jessica regretted even saying anything. She should have kept her stupid mouth shut.

"Shut up!" Alana said, her surprised exclamation startling her. "That's amazing."

Jessica relaxed as Rebecca also leaned close. "Yeah, you should teach us how," Rebecca added, as excited as the other woman was.

"Hell, yeah," Brett concurred, putting an arm around his wife. "I'd be all right with that."

The table broke into laughter and Jessica relaxed a little more. But she tensed again when she saw Rafael and Alex standing in a far corner. They looked deep into a tense conversation. She wondered what they were talking about. The last thing she wanted to do was to come between Rafael and his oldest friend. It was an intense moment, and she wanted to leave the table, just for a moment, so she could breathe.

"If you guys will just excuse me for a moment, I need to go to the ladies' room." She stood, and left the table. Even as she walked away, she could feel their eyes on her back.

"What is your fucking problem?" Rafael asked Alex, when they were alone. He was pissed, but on a night as important as the masquerade, they couldn't appear to be fighting in front of their guests.

"I don't have a problem," Alex maintained. "But what I do have is a healthy curiosity." He raised his hands. "What the hell is going on? Why did you bring Jessica here?"

"Because I wanted to. I wanted her to be here with me."

"So, are you guys dating or something?" Rafael didn't know how to answer the question. "Dude, we tell each other everything. You haven't been the same since you got back from San Francisco, and I can only assume it's because of Jessica. What's going on with the two of you?"

"Okay, just keep your voice down. We are sleeping together."

"That's old news. Tell me something I don't know. And I don't want this *nothing* bullshit. You think I don't know you better than you know yourself? How long have we known each other?"

"Too long," Rafael responded stubbornly.

"Since kindergarten, man. We've been through a lot together. And I don't know why you won't trust me with whatever is going on with you and Jessica."

Rafael blew out a heavy breath. Tired of lying and avoiding his feelings, he was weary. And for weeks, he'd just thought Alex was pissed at him for jeopardizing the campaign, but he could also see that his friend was hurt by being shut out. "I don't know. I never thought it would go this far. It's like I'm going crazy. She makes me forget that we're opponents. That the last thing on my mind should be sex, or her, or how I feel when I'm with her."

"No," Alex said quietly. "Because I need you to keep focused on the job, and getting elected. If this is just sex, fine, relieve a little tension when you need to. But not with her. Jessica has the power to destroy everything you've worked for."

"What, you're giving me orders now? You don't get to dictate who I sleep with."

"No, I don't. But I never thought you'd be so fucking reckless. So, what are you doing now? Throwing the campaign so she'll win?"

"Hell no," he responded, adamant. "I know how important the office is to all of us."

"Do you think she's using you, to distract you from the election?"

"Not a chance."

Alex was silent, and he nodded, taking in what Rafael had just told him. "That's all well and good. But I'm going to play bad cop here for a minute. I'm not your best friend now, I'm your campaign manager, and it's my job to make sure you win this election. Did you see the latest poll numbers?"

He knew by Alex's tone that they probably weren't good, and he turned his back. "No."

"You're down again. By four points."

"Fuck."

"You really need to get your head back in the game, man. You've only got a couple weeks before the election. It's crunch time. You have to hit the trail hard. Without worrying about getting your dick wet in your opponent, no matter how much you might like her. Do you even care about winning anymore?"

"Of course I do," Rafael hissed. "No matter what's going on between me and Jessica, I'm going to put it aside. You know me, I'll do anything I need to win."

Rafael saw Alex's gaze rise to a point behind him, over his shoulder. He turned around and Jessica standing behind him. He blinked quickly. He hadn't heard her come up behind him. "Hey, what's up? Is everything okay?"

"Yeah, I was just on my way back from the restroom." Her tone gave nothing away. Had she heard any part of their conversation? His proclamation that he would do anything to win?

When she left Rafael and made it back to the table, the previous conversation had resumed. It seemed as if his friends still had questions for her.

"So, I'm guessing that with your rising political career, you can't keep dancing, right?" Gabe said to her.

"What did I miss over here?" She looked up and saw that Rafael had made his way back up the platform. He reclaimed his seat next to her. But she noticed that he was alone. Alex was nowhere to be found.

"Jessica was just telling us about her side job."

"Oh, really?" he asked, obviously surprised.

"I've got an idea," Alana said. "Why don't you do a performance here?"

She felt Rafael's gaze on her. "I don't know. In Las Vegas? I can't. People will see that it's me."

"It's so perfect, though. You're a world-champion dancer, it'd be a great show for our guests."

Jessica looked to Rafael, who was still watching her, his face unreadable. He'd already made it known that he didn't like the idea of her dancing. What did he make of his friend's offer?

"Absolutely not," he said.

"Why not?" Alana asked.

"I don't dance in Vegas," Jessica told her. "Someone could see me, they'll say something."

"They're legally not allowed to say anything. It's in the contract," Gabe reminded her. "You could wear a mask."

"Maybe." She was still unsure, and she looked around the table at the expectant eyes. Rafael's were the only ones that said he disapproved.

"We have a stage, and we have regular shows and performances here in the main room," Gabe offered.

"Yeah, I'll arrange everything for you." Alana pulled out her phone and consulted the screen, scrolling down several times, until she looked up again. "How's Friday?"

"Friday?" she asked, her mind racing. She had at least one million things to do. The election was scheduled for the following week. Dancing would be the perfect way to expel all the tension and energy that would bring. But she shook her head. What was she afraid of? She danced all the time, and she knew she would miss it when she had to quit. Perhaps Di Terrestres would give her a chance. She smiled. It would be fine. But as she looked at Rafael, a small niggling of suspicion formed in her stomach, and she remembered what she'd overheard him say to Alex. *I'll do anything to win.*

Oh, whatever. Friday would give her almost a week to come up with a routine, and the opportunity to perform would be welcome.

"I don't think this is a good idea," Rafael muttered. She could tell he wasn't happy about it, but she'd about made up her mind, and Rafael wasn't going to tell her no if she wanted to do something.

She looked up at Rafael and put a hand on his thigh and squeezed, as he covered it with his own. It felt like a perfectly regular moment between two lovers. But their relationship was nothing close to regular. She shut her eyes and tried to remind herself that they weren't in a relationship, and whatever it was, they had to end it or risk exposure. "I'll do it."

Rafael grimaced, but she ignored him. With the matter put to bed, everyone began to engage in their own conversations. Jessica leaned back in her chair, and into Rafael, stroking her fingers up and down his thigh, until she felt him relax under her touch. His arm wrapped around her, and with his fingertips, he drew circles over her bare back. "Let's go for a walk."

They walked down into the party. "I know you don't want me to perform, but you said you wanted to see me dance again."

"I know, but part of me doesn't want anyone else to see you."

She opened her mouth to respond, to tell him that he couldn't boss her around, but instead she stopped when someone over his shoulder caught her attention. "Oh, my God," she whispered.

"What?"

She pointed at a woman in the crowd. She wore a small mask over her eyes, but it was obvious who it was. "It's Tanya Roberts. From LVTV."

"Shit," Rafael muttered. "How did she get in? We

have a strict no-press rule, even if they're not attending in the capacity of a reporter.

"It's okay. I'll get Alana to see whose guest she is, and revoke his privileges for life. And if she says anything, or if anything pops up about us, we bring her down. Hard."

"It isn't okay. We can't be here together. In your freaking sex club." She tried to catch her breath. She knew it wasn't a good idea to go. She'd known better. "I want to leave."

"Okay. Where do you want to go?"

"I want to go home."

He nodded. "Okay, I'll take you."

Rafael's teeth gnashed together as the driver made his way to Jessica's home. They'd left immediately, but not before he'd relayed to Alana and the rest of the club management that a well-known reporter had made her way inside.

"This is it," Jessica said as he approached her house, and he pulled his SUV into her narrow driveway. The ride from the club had been quiet. The party had been a shit show on every level. He'd fought with Alex, a reporter had probably seen them there together. And now it had put distance between him and Jessica. He could feel the chasm widen between them with every second that passed.

"I'm going to walk you in."

She sighed. "If you insist."

On their way to the front door, he put his hand on

her back, and as she fumbled for her keys, he looked up and down the street, his senses heightened, trying to see if anyone was watching them. He didn't think so. But they couldn't be too careful. If Tanya had seen them together, there was no stopping her from looking at them more closely.

She fit her key in the door, and Rafael feared that if he let her enter her house alone, he would never get her back. His fingertips spread over the bare skin. "I'm really sorry about how tonight turned out."

"Me, too." She looked around, paranoid, surveying their surroundings as if she was also checking for reporters. "We shouldn't stick around out here for too long."

"You going to invite me in?"

She stepped back. "Come on in," she said, without much emotion.

He closed the door behind them, and he turned the lock. "What's wrong?"

"Nothing."

"You aren't a very good liar."

"I'm just tired, I guess."

"Do you want me to leave?"

Jessica sighed. Part of her did want Rafael to leave. But the part that wanted him to stay, the womanly part of her, won out. She reached for the lapels of his shirt, pulled him to her and kissed him. She might be conflicted about how she felt about him, but that didn't mean she didn't want him.

Rafael cupped her hips and pulled her close. He kicked the door closed and flipped the dead bolt. Taking control, he pushed her to the wall, and kissed her roughly, before turning her so that she was facing away from him, and he pressed his crotch into her ass. He must have also felt the vibration because a low growl emitted from his throat—a lustful sound that turned her on even further.

Rafael pulled her closer. "Are you mad at me?"

"Generally, always."

His chuckle washed over her, as his hands ran down her back and palmed her ass. He squeezed and she pressed closer against him. She forgot about being suspicious of him, and she hated herself for how weak his touch, and the promise of more, made her. What sort of strong, independent woman did that make her? "Let's go to bed."

Jessica could feel his heart pounding against her chest, as his hands grazed up her thighs, trailing up the hem of her dress.

"Where's your bedroom?"

Jessica led Rafael up the staircase to her bedroom. She was relieved to see Ben's open door, which told her that they were alone in the house. She opened the door to her own room and turned the lights on low, giving the room an intimate glow. He came up behind her and put his lips on the back of her neck, and she leaned against him as he kissed the sensitive skin there.

"Damn," he muttered against her electrified skin. "I don't have a condom. Do you have any?"

"Uh, yeah." She reached into the nightstand. "Here."

"Perfect." He lowered the straps on her gown. "I love this dress." Her breasts kept her dress up and he pushed the material down to sit at her hips. She was braless underneath, and he reached around and cupped her, pinching her nipples, forcing a gasp from her. She leaned back against him and he kissed her neck. Gripping her hips and turning her to face him, he took her lips with his own. Where their kisses had always been frantic, frenzied, this one was different. He kissed her softly, reverently, as he lowered her to the mattress, not taking his lips from hers.

He pushed her dress over her hips, and quickly shucked his own clothing. Soon they were both naked, washing their hands over each other. Jessica couldn't get enough of his smooth skin, hard muscles, coarse dark hair. He settled between her legs, her thighs bracketing his waist, as if he was built to fit there. Rafael was perfect. Perfect for her.

He reached for the condoms and, with sure hands, rolled the latex over himself and pushed inside of her, filling her. It was such a familiar feeling now. But she wanted more. She lifted her hips, meeting his thrusts. He lifted his face from his place in the crook of her neck, and his eyes found hers. Locking on her eyes, he continued his steady pace, stoking the fires within her into an inferno that threatened to consume her, when she realized that this time with Rafael was different. She wrapped her arms around his neck and pulled him closer, kissing him deeply. Her heartbeat stuttered as she realized that it was different because it wasn't just sex, rough, reckless, the scratching of an itch. Jessica realized that she had some kind of feelings for him. *Could it be love?*

"Ah, *mami*," he whispered, the tone sending a shiver up her spine. "You feel so good." His moan rang through the room, and hers joined it. They were both close, but she knew that he was holding back until she finished.

"Just let go, Raf," she whispered, pushing back against him. It was all he needed, and something in him snapped, his pace increased, but he kept his arms around her, holding her close. His hand reached down to where they were joined and he circled his fingers around her clit, providing her with exactly what she needed. The slow burn of pleasure spread, and the heat radiated throughout her body. The inferno consumed her, and she cried out. Rafael's yells mixed with her own, as they focused on nothing but each other, and chasing their mutual pleasure. He stilled over her, and his weight was pleasant, and she drew lazy circles on his back with her fingernails.

Rafael moved away from her to dispose of the condom, and when he returned to her bed, he pulled the rumpled comforter over them both and held her close. He wrapped his arms around her while she sprawled over his chest. She could hear and feel his pounding heartbeat against her cheek, and she reveled in the feeling of being wrapped up in him. She didn't want to admit it to herself. It made her life so much more complicated.

"You're incredible, Jess," he whispered into her hair.

She hummed in response. "You're not so shabby yourself." One thing rang through her mind, rousing her from the postcoital haze. "What happens if she releases a story about us?"

She felt his arms tighten around her. He planted his lips on the side of her head, while his fingertips trailed down her spine. "She won't. I'll see to it."

"This is stupid, isn't it?"

"Yeah, it is, but I can't help myself around you."

"Same," she said, snuggling closer to him. When she pulled herself close to him, everything felt right. Her heart pounded, and her chest clenched as she struggled to breathe. She knew the signs. Whether she wanted to or not, she was falling in love with Rafael Martinez.

CHAPTER THIRTEEN

"COUNCILMAN MARTINEZ, do you have time for a few words?"

Rafael turned away from the Wednesday afternoon festivities to face the woman who'd spoken to him. He had only a couple of minutes before he had to be at the front of the crowd for the official opening of a new community center.

The Brotherhood had anonymously been behind the revitalization of the state-of-the-art facility, which included a playground and swimming pools as well as after-school and arts programs. It would be a great addition to the community, and while Rafael wasn't officially one of the benefactors *on paper*, he had been instrumental in getting the project through city council, as some councillors had tried to block it in favor of a parking lot. It was something that he and Jessica had agreed on. They'd fought it and won.

"For you, Tanya, anything," he said, and smiled at the reporter, then the cameraman setting up the shot behind them.

Tanya smiled back, giving no indication that she'd seen them together at the past weekend's masquerade party. Turning toward the camera, she said, "As someone who has spent a decade in municipal politics, how do you explain Jessica Morgan's sudden popularity, after just two years on city council? It seems like she's been giving you a run for your money."

He looked over Tanya's shoulder and saw Jessica standing in the crowd, greeting onlookers. She was campaigning, but he knew that really she was connecting to the people, and she wasn't just there as a politician. Jessica cared about them, and he admired that. Smiling and laughing with her constituents, she was stunning. Watching her made his chest clench with need. He just wanted to be with her.

"I'm going to be honest, she's definitely kept me on my toes." He chuckled. "But being part of this mayoral race has been so rewarding—especially as it's captured the interest and imagination of the public so intensely." Rafael smiled at the reporters now gathered around him. Despite that his words were true, the pressure was on. He and Jessica had to be careful within the public eye, but being careful was becoming harder, as he found himself growing more and more desperate for her.

Tanya leaned in. "Well, look at you guys," she replied. "You're both young, attractive. At a time when people are paying attention to politics, you're both very interesting. You're making the story sexy," she said with a wink.

"I guess you've got a point there," he started, before turning back on the *politician*. "And I'm extremely grateful that the people of Las Vegas have taken such a great interest in municipal politics and what happens in their city."

"And what are your thoughts on Jessica Morgan?"

Besides the fact that she's sex on stilettos, with a sweet ass? "As for Ms. Morgan, I'm honestly very surprised by her popularity. She's proven to be quite a fierce opponent. She has a passion, which I believe is resonating with many in the city. Although, she's relatively unqualified and has so little experience in municipal politics, and while I believe that she is an excellent councillor at city hall, I just don't believe her to be capable of taking the mayor's seat."

"How do you think she's going to react to you calling her unqualified?"

He smiled. "Well, it's a factual statement. Whether or not she'll like it, that remains to be seen," he finished smoothly before turning away. He *knew* that Jessica wouldn't like it. But maybe she wouldn't be too angry about it. He smirked again, thinking about her possible retaliation. *Like hell she won't.*

He tried to maintain his poker face, but it was difficult. He was finding it harder and harder to school his emotions and separate his feelings about Jessica. He'd woken up with his arms around her, and for several minutes that morning, he'd just watched her sleep, the delicate rise and fall of her chest, and when her eyelids fluttered open, he kissed her, without saying a word, and then made love to her again. *Made love.* Was that what he'd been doing? He already felt more strongly tied to Jessica than he'd ever felt with a woman. But was it love? He shook himself free of the memories when he realized that Tanya was still looking at him.

He smiled and started to move away, but Tanya stopped him again. "Just one more question. A source tells me that you are a part-owner in Di Terrestres, a well-known, members-only, erotic club, and that you're also heavily involved in the other business activities of its owners. What do you say about a potential conflict of interest seeing as how you want to be mayor?"

That made Rafael pause. "A *source* told you?" He could imagine there being no source, and that Tanya had followed her own hunch. "Tanya, I assure you and the citizens of Las Vegas that there is no conflict of interest in my campaign. I did have interest in several businesses, but that is in a blind trust. I'm no longer in control of the management of them. My only connection to Di Terrestres is that I have office space in the same building." He lied easily. "If I were you, I'd check my sources."

"That's your official statement?"

He nodded. "Absolutely."

Tanya didn't look convinced, but she extended her hand and he shook it. "Okay, thank you, councilman. Good luck with the campaign."

"Anytime," he told her, knowing that she hadn't been placated, and that he would have to think quickly and do some damage control. He walked away from her and again saw Jessica working the crowd. Tanya had somehow gotten into the club the other night, but could it have been Jessica who'd tipped her off? He'd told her about his ownership in the club when few other people knew, and she had the most to gain from this getting leaked. *Was* it her?

"Fuck," he muttered, as he walked toward some business leaders who were waving to him. He had work to do. He took another look at Jessica over his shoulder. He should warn her about Tanya's source. But he didn't have time at the moment. He had work to do.

"Unqualified?" Jessica laughed, incredulously, at Tanya Roberts, who'd stopped her. "He said I was unqualified?"

Tanya spoke into the mic. "He also said that you were 'not capable of taking the mayor's seat.' What are your thoughts?"

"I think this is another example of Councilman Martinez being unable to look past his own ego. He thinks that if one isn't a successful, influential man, then they aren't fit to lead. My commitment to the job and the people of Las Vegas is unmatched by Mr. Martinez."

"But how do you intend to lead the city with such little political experience."

"In my two years on council, I've been doing the work and paying attention. I've researched, studied. I've attended city hall council meetings, and I've worked closely with the current mayor, so I know what the job entails. But I believe that my lack of political experience will serve the city better, because I *haven't* spent years cultivating relationships that require earning and doing favors. I'm not here to play a game. I don't have any political allegiances to anyone besides the people of Las Vegas," she finished. "Think you've got some good sound bites there?"

"I believe I do," Tanya said, offering her hand. Jessica shook it and turned back to the festivities. She watched the kids play, her mind wondering what Rafael's response to her statements would be.

When Tanya walked away, Jessica looked into the crowd and saw Rafael, talking with another councillor. She pulled out her phone and typed a message to him.

Unqualified, huh?

She watched as he reached into the breast pocket of his sports coat and pulled out his phone. He looked at the screen, and she smiled when he threw his head back in laughter. He shook the hand of the councillor and walked away, putting the phone to his ear. Her own phone rang in her hand and she answered.

"I said *relatively unqualified,*" he said when she raised the phone to her ear.

"Is that right?" She laughed. "How about being incapable of taking the mayor's seat?" she challenged.

"Okay, yeah, I might have said that."

"You're so dead."

"Do you think we can get out of here anytime soon?"

"What do you have in mind?"

"Why don't we go to Di Terrestres tonight? So we know we can have a little privacy. I want to be with you."

She had work to do that night, arranging some final interviews and appearances before the election. Her to-do list was pages long with the things she'd been neglecting because of Rafael. Not to mention the performance she'd agreed to give at the club. But an invitation from him made her forget all of that. He did something to her, made her forget absolutely everything of importance. It was frustrating, and for someone who tried so hard to keep her wits about her, to be independent and strong, an atomic bomb could have gone off outside the room, and she knew it would not part them. She closed her eyes and mustered all of her strength. "I can't. I have work to do."

"So do I."

That sounded good to her. It felt like with the closeness of the election, the press's increased presence in their lives was starting to seem intrusive. She didn't know what would happen if their relationship—or whatever it was—was discovered. "What time should I show up?"

"Why don't you come by around eight?"

"Okay," she said again, with a smile. With just a couple of words, he'd made her completely change her mind. She seemed to be smiling more when she thought of Rafael, as crazy as he made her. "I'll see you then." She hung up the phone and so did he. Jessica looked around, and her smile fell when she and Tanya locked eyes, before the other woman's also found Rafael, who, oblivious, was putting his phone in his pocket.

Tanya's smile left Jessica feeling cold. The reporter had always been so kind to Jessica, gave her the opportunity to speak on air, but now as she saw the kernels of an explosive story form behind her eyes, Jessica went into full-fledged panic. She wanted to get out of there, but first, she had to figure out what Tanya was thinking. She smiled and, holding her head high, walked over to Tanya.

"This is going to be a great addition to the neighborhood," Jessica said, when she approached the other woman. "It really will be a fantastic spot."

"Indeed," Tanya said. "I'm just wondering, Jessica. We don't know a lot about you, your personal life. Are you seeing anyone?"

"Are we on the record?" Jessica asked.

"I'm always on the record."

"Well, in that case, no. I'm not seeing anyone."

Jessica maintained eye contact, but she knew that Tanya wasn't convinced. The other woman watched her carefully, until she nodded and shook Jessica's hand. "Until next time," Tanya said. "Keep in touch. If there's anything you want to tell me, please call."

"Will do," Jessica told her, and she watched Tanya walk away.

Jessica's heart pounded in her chest. Tanya was on to them—she knew it. They were too close, to each other, to the election. The stakes had never been higher for either of them. She was already committed to perform at Di Terrrestres the upcoming weekend, but she knew she should keep her distance until then, no matter how difficult it was.

Her phone was still in her hand, and she opened Rafael's contact information. No matter how badly she wanted to see him that night, she had to protect herself.

She typed out a quick message to him. *I can't meet you tonight. I'll see you Friday, when I perform.* And then she turned off her phone, put it in her purse and made her way from the festivities, before he even had a chance to respond.

CHAPTER FOURTEEN

JESSICA TOOK A deep breath, as she stood behind the curtains of the stage that had been erected in the club. As Rafael had told her, the floor, normally used for dancing, rose into a platform for performances. The club had installed a pole in the middle and new stage lights just for her. She still felt a niggling of doubt about her interactions with Tanya Roberts, but she'd been assured by Alana that she would be fine. There was nothing to worry about. Cell phones would be collected at the door, and no member of the press would be admitted, under any circumstance. She was safer at Di Terrestres than anywhere else.

"Hey, are you ready?" Alana came up to her. "Everything is ready to go for you."

"Yeah, I definitely am. I'm nervous, though. More nervous than I've ever been," she admitted, tightening the mask over her eyes. "I guess it's because I've never been the only one performing. There have always been other women sharing the stage."

"Ladies and gentlemen," the club's announcer

started. "Get ready, because you are in for a treat. Making her first, and only, appearance at Di Terrestres is world pole-dancing champion, Jessie M."

Her music started, and she pushed past the curtains and onto the stage. The room quieted, as dozens of eyes stared rapturously at her. She loved that part, holding the audience in her hand as they watched her every movement, owning the stage. She loved it, and it loved her.

For that evening's more dramatic act, she'd worn a long flowing black silk skirt, which matched the lace mask that covered the top half of her face. Her hair was curled and piled in a gravity-defying style high on her head, courtesy of the hair and makeup artist that Alana had arranged for her. For her performance, she'd worked with the in-house DJ and created a medley of songs, starting with sultry music that had a slow, driving drumbeat and then progressed into faster dance music. That way, she could give the audience a taste of each of her routines.

She did her best sexy strut across the stage, on precariously high stilettos that lengthened her already long legs. She looked and felt incredible. She danced toward the pole, her movements seductive. Even with the lights shining in her face, and the eyes of every patron on her, she could still look around the room and find Rafael, sitting at his usual table with his friends. She was surprised that he would support her in the career he didn't approve of, and that he would sit by and watch as she took off her clothes in front of others. Everything she knew about the man told her that he didn't share well.

But he and everyone else kept watching as she ripped away her dress to reveal the sexy, black sheer bodysuit she'd worn under her gown. The music changed and sped up, her cue to approach the pole. Giving a couple of cursory spins around the pole, seductively spreading her legs, grinding against it, she then got down to the work that had won her many awards around the world.

Grasping higher up on the pole, she spun again, this time pulling her legs from the floor, letting her upper-body and core strength, and the momentum of her arms, swing her around the pole. Then, keeping her arms in the same position, she inverted her body, so that she was holding herself upside down. She heard some impressed gasps over the music, and she smiled at their reaction.

You haven't seen anything yet.

She wrapped her legs around the pole. Gripping it with her thighs and using her abdominal muscles, and even now, still spinning, she sat upright. Then, she grabbed the metal with her hands and performed a split before contorting herself around the pole so that it rested in the curve of her lower back. With her legs still split, and circling the bar as if she were a perpetual motion machine, she took one ankle and held it near her head. She continued to spin down the pole in lazy, languid circles, her speed decreasing until her lower foot hit the floor. The lights went out as the music ended.

Jessica gathered her breath, and let her spent muscles contract, as the room erupted into thunderous applause. She took a bow, blew a kiss to the audience and left the stage.

Alana stopped her first, and handed her a bottle of water. It was just what she needed. "Oh, my God, that was amazing!"

"Thanks," Jessica said, before gratefully gulping back the water.

Alana took a covert look around to make sure they were alone. "God, Rafael said that you've won championships, but, girl, pole dancing should be in the Olympics. Do you think you could show me some moves?"

"Yeah, definitely. Let's get together sometime." She looked past Alana to see Rafael coming toward her. His gait was rigid, his eyes were dark and she knew the one thing that was on his mind—her. Alana glanced over and saw him approach before she turned back to Jessica. "Well, I guess I'll see you later." She walked away, and patted Rafael on the chest in greeting without actually speaking. If he noticed her, he didn't say anything.

"What'd you think?" she asked.

The water bottle she'd held in her hand crashed to the floor, as he pulled her to him, almost whipping her to his chest. His response was a kiss so heated, so demanding that she couldn't breathe as his tongue struck into her, plundering, fighting hers for domination. He pushed her to the wall and kissed her senseless until he pulled away.

"Fuck, that was so goddamn hot, I could barely stand it," he muttered low against her lips. She could feel his cock, hard steel against her, and she rubbed against it.

"I didn't think I could watch you take off your clothes in front of a room of strangers again, but I couldn't take my eyes off you."

"I kind of thought you would change your mind. Cancel my appearance. Tell Alana I wouldn't do it. Just so no one would be able to see me."

"I'll admit. I was close," he said with a smile. "But I'm so glad I didn't. You're beautiful, talented, and while everyone in that room wanted you, only I know how smooth your skin really is," he said, trailing his fingers down her arms before pinching a loose tendril of hair. "Or what it's like to twine my fingers in your hair, and what it's like to have your thighs wrapped around me like that pole. The sounds you make when you're turned on, and what it feels like to push inside of you and fuck you until you scream," he finished, his lips against the overcharged nerve endings of her neck.

Rafael seduced her with his words, her body threatened to orgasm just with his breath on her skin, and she moaned.

"Although, there's one thing I don't know."

"What's that?"

"You told me that night at Charlie's that you don't give private dances, but I'm dying to know what it's like to have you dance for only me."

"You want a dance?"

"More than anything."

Jessica thought about it and decided there was no way she wouldn't dance for the man in front of her. She took his hand. "Let's go."

"We can go to my room. It's private." Lacing his fingers with hers, he led her away from the backstage area, and to the staircase that led to the exclusive suites.

When they entered his, she went to the sound system and selected a song. A slow, steady, sexy beat that would allow her to get up close and personal.

Feeling the song's pulse course through her, she sauntered over to him. His eyes were molten, his nostrils flared, and she looked down and saw the bulge in his lap, tenting his pants. All telltale signs that he was as turned on as she was.

She put her hands on the arms of the large chair, and leaned over Rafael, letting her breasts come within a hair's breadth of his chest.

Jessica backed up, and then turned around so that her ass was to him, and she bent forward, thrusting her ass in his direction, until she heard his low growl, which told her the moves were successful. She turned to face him and dropped to the floor, spreading her legs, and then pushed back up to a standing position.

Kneeling on the chair, straddling his thighs, she ground herself against him. He was hard and hot, and she wanted him. She reached between their bodies and grasped his hard cock and rubbed him through his pants. He closed his eyes and moaned as his hands cupped her hips. She whipped them away. "You can't touch."

"Why not?"

"Those are the rules," she told him. "No touching."

"I guess I forgot. Why don't you just keep touching me, then?"

"My pleasure," she told him. The music forgotten, she slipped off the chair and settled on the floor between his knees. She unbuttoned his jeans, reached into them and pulled out his cock. It was hard and pulsed in her hand. A drop of pre-cum crested the top and she leaned in and collected it with her mouth, the saltiness lingering there. Not taking her gaze from his heavy-hooded stare, she flattened her tongue against the bottom of his erection and ran it up the sensitive underside, and then swiped it around his crown before taking him fully into her mouth. She took him deeply enough to feel him hit the back of her throat, and then slowly drew her head back, almost releasing him, before swallowing him again.

His hand found the back of her head, his fingers twining in her hair, guiding her pace. "Fuck, Jessica," he muttered. His breath was a hiss between his teeth. His breathing quickened, and she knew he was close, but he pushed her away. He reached out and grabbed her, seated her in his lap.

He took a condom from his pocket and held it out to her. She took it, ripped the foil package open and rolled the latex over him. His jaw was tense as he fought for control, and her fingers on him hadn't much helped matters. Gripping his base, she aligned him with her sopping wet, needy opening and she seated herself fully over him.

As she moved her hips, riding him, he kept pace,

thrusting into her. Her body was so swollen with desire, so ready that within just a couple of minutes, she found herself cresting, climbing higher and higher, until she reached the top. She felt like she was floating above herself, watching herself as she rode Rafael's lap. Until with one final thrust, she felt herself leap off the edge, and his loud groan told her that Rafael had jumped with her. They stilled, and out of breath, layered in sweat, Jessica and Rafael watched each other. She felt a tightness in her chest.

Jessica smiled, inhaling his scent deeply. His sweat and cologne together were a strong aphrodisiac, and as spent as she was, she couldn't help herself from wanting him again.

He continued to gaze at her. "You're amazing. But what happens in a couple of days?"

"The election."

He nodded.

"I don't know. I guess we should just wait and see what happens. We'll see who wins, and then we'll just have a difficult conversation about what happens next." Jessica knew she was in love with the man who was holding her. Her heart broke in two thinking about not being with him. But no matter what happened, she would go about her life without him, if she needed to, and forget the nights they'd spent together.

"I guess we'll just wait to see, then," he said, and she didn't miss the way his arms tightened around her. She looked up at him, and saw that his eyes were as busy and anguished as hers, and that there were words he was leaving unsaid.

Jessica snuggled closer, but she was transported back to the real world. The election was next week, and whatever was on Rafael's mind threatened to put their night to an end. She didn't want it to. She wanted to stay in their cocoon, just a little longer, so she closed her eyes and rested against him, and listened to the sound of his breathing.

CHAPTER FIFTEEN

"Mr. Martinez," Jillian buzzed through Rafael's office. It was after hours, and as usual, he had continued working out of his office in the BH building. "Tanya Roberts from LVTV is here to see you."

"I don't have an appointment with her, do I?"

"No, you don't. But she insisted on seeing you."

"All right, send her in." He stood to greet Tanya, curious as to why she would come by his office. "Ms. Roberts," he said to her when she entered, shaking her hand. "How are you this evening?"

"I'm great, and you?"

"Busy," he said pointedly. "With the election in a few days, there's a lot of last-minute things to get done. What can I do for you?"

"I'm here to give you a heads-up. Tomorrow, I'm going to run a story about you and Jessica Morgan."

Rafael's heart raced, but he tried to not let it show. "What kind of story?"

"One that details a romantic relationship between the two of you."

Rafael scoffed. "That's ridiculous. I would have expected more from a reporter of your caliber."

"I searched through some back photos of you both and it seems as if there's some chemistry between you."

"That's ludicrous, and it gives you nothing," he insisted.

"Is it?" she asked, producing a tablet, and she scrolled through several photos of them at public events, during what they thought had been private moments, where they'd been captured leaning close. They'd only been talking, but he recognized the way they looked at each other. Like the lovers they were.

"Is this all you've got?" he asked her. "I'm not overly impressed by your scoop, if you only have photos of us talking. You'll have to try harder."

She scrolled across to another photo, one of them embracing, outside his home, as he ushered her inside. He was holding her close, his hand settled on the curve of her ass. *Not great, but it could definitely be worse.*

His fists clenched at his thighs, and he had to step away from the woman so that he wouldn't whip the tablet from her fingers and fling it across the room.

"And there's also this."

He looked and saw a picture of Jessica entering Di Terrestres the other night before her show. "And I've got more salacious video and photos of her. She's quite the dancer, isn't she? Among other things…" Tanya raised a knowing eyebrow. "Plus, a little digging told me that you are indeed one of the owners of that club. You've been removed from the books, but you still own an equal amount of interest, as does each of your friends. What do you have to say about you being romantically involved with your opposition in the mayoral race?"

He sobered. "How did you get these?"

"I have my sources."

"Son of a bitch," he muttered to himself. "What do you want?"

"Whatever do you mean?"

"You came here for a reason instead of just running with it."

She shrugged. "I am going to run the story. But I wanted your reaction first."

"Has Jessica seen it?"

"Not yet. I came straight to you. I only waited in taking it to Jessica because I've also been doing some deeper research involving a strip club in San Francisco."

"Why are you doing this? The election is this week."

"And this is one hell of a story, don't you think? Breaking this will launch my career into national news."

"By reporting on our personal lives? I think you've got a great tabloid journalism career ahead of you. Maybe TMZ is hiring." He met her eyes directly. "I thought you were credible. But you should know that the minute you leave my office, my lawyers will be on you. It's over. This story won't see the light of day."

"You'd better hurry, then. In this day and age, a lot can happen in a couple of minutes."

But Rafael didn't fear her. He'd tangled with adversaries far more frightening to him than some local reporter. "Sure can. To both of us."

"Is that a threat?"

He shrugged.

Tanya smirked. "Good luck, councillor," she said, before turning and walking out of his office.

CHAPTER SIXTEEN

JESSICA FOUND OUT about it when the rest of world did. She had been given no advance notice, no call from the news stations that had picked it up, and she was preparing her dinner when the news broke. She saw the television screen flash pictures of both her and Rafael, followed by a video clip of a woman giving a man a lap dance. She recognized the room before she recognized the people. It was her. And Rafael. The night they'd gone to his private room at Di Terrestres. Then a video played of her onstage performance that night.

She dropped her wineglass on the floor, the glass shattered on the hardwood, splashing red wine all over everything.

"No, no, no, no…" she whispered to the television as a cold shock completely stilled her. She watched herself on camera, gyrating over Rafael's lap, her hand reaching down to grab him, before she slid to her knees in front of him. Luckily the video stopped there. But not soon enough to halt the sheer damage that had been done in twenty seconds.

"A source close to the story has confirmed that may-oral candidate Jessica Morgan is also an exotic dancer."

A source close to the story?

Her cell phone rang. Panicked, she picked it up. "Hello?"

"Ms. Morgan? This is Terrance Beady, Tanya Rob-erts's PA from LVTV News, do you have any comment on the sex tape that has been leaked, showing you and Councilman Martinez in a compromising situation?"

"Uh, no, no comment," she stammered, before hang-ing up the phone. She looked at the screen. In the sec-onds that she had been on the phone, she had already missed ten phone calls, and the voice mail notifica-tion listed corresponding messages. Still in her hand, the phone rang again. Startled, she tossed it aside. The world had gotten ahold of the most private things in her life, and it was running with it.

"Jessie, I heard something break." Ben came up be-hind her from his room. He looked her over. "Oh, my God, what's wrong?" He went to her and wrapped his arms around her.

She could barely speak, so she just shook her head, buried her face in the crook of his shoulder and cried. He asked nothing of her, apparently willing to wait until she told him what was wrong.

When she finally felt cried out, Jessica pulled back and picked up her phone. The notifications had more than tripled. People were still trying to reach her. But a quick look told her that none of them was Rafael. She opened her internet browser and, with no trouble, she found a link to the video and showed her friend.

He took her phone and watched the screen. "Is that you? And Rafael? Oh, my God, where did this come from? Who leaked it?"

"I don't know."

"Did he?"

"I don't know. I wouldn't have thought so, but we were in his room, in his club. He had to have known that camera was there. I know he'd do anything to win." It dawned on her. That was exactly what he'd said to Alex that night she'd overheard him at Di Terrestres.

"Son of a bitch."

It all started to make sense. He must be in on this with Tanya. This must be why nothing had ever come of finding out how Tanya had gotten into the masquerade party. It was why he'd let her dance at his club. He'd set her up, recorded her. Then fucked her and leaked the tape so she'd drop out of the race. She felt stupid, betrayed. He'd earned her trust, and then he'd broken it. She'd loved him. But she had to pull herself back together. She had work to do.

"Why don't you call him?" Ben asked.

"I don't have time. I've got to meet with my team. I've got to get ahead of this."

The next morning, Rafael had to fight his way through the throngs of reporters outside of the BH before he entered the office building that evening. "What do you have to say about your relationship with Jessica Morgan?"

Rafael paused but didn't fully stop. He didn't need the press to see him falter. He knew that the story was out, but he had no idea how exactly to respond to it. He pushed through the doors and saw Alex and Jillian waiting for him, pacing, looking none too happy. "Well, that didn't take long." The story had exploded overnight.

"I've been trying to call you," Alex said, striding over to him.

"I was stuck in traffic and I left my phone at home. I forgot it in my rush to get here."

"You should have just stayed home. Any press camping out outside your place?" Alex asked.

"Of course there was," he said.

"Have you been talking to Jessica?"

He shook his head. "She won't answer any of my calls. And I went by her place last night. She wasn't home." He straightened, he had to get back into business mode. He had work to do. "How bad is it?"

"It's bad. There's a video of you guys in your suite. It cuts off before it gets too scandalous. But there aren't any questions what happened next," Alex said, passing over his phone. The screen showed a news website. His picture was profiled along with Jessica's. The headline screamed Las Vegas Mayoral Candidates' Steamy Romp in Sex Club.

He pushed Play and saw a video of him sitting on a couch and Jessica dancing for him. He didn't have to keep watching to know that it was from Friday, right before they'd had sex in his suite at Di Terrestres. "Oh, God. Where the fuck did the tape come from?"

"I have no fucking idea."

"How can we stop this?" He looked between Alex and Jillian, who hadn't spoken yet and wouldn't maintain eye contact.

"It's going to be tough," Alex told him. "We'll call Gabe, see if we can get an injunction against the websites to take it down. But that doesn't mean it hasn't already been downloaded and seen by God knows how many people. It's already been retweeted, reblogged and shared thousands of times on Facebook."

"Fuck," he muttered. "This happened at Di Terrestres. We need to find out who put a camera in my room, and when we do, we take them down." He leaned in to the group. "And I wouldn't be surprised if Tanya Roberts set up this video herself, just to give credit to her story."

"That's not possible, is it?" Jillian asked. "Di Terrestres has impeccable security."

"She somehow got into the masquerade. Gabe's been looking into it, but Tanya likely saw us together, then somehow got into my room and left the camera." He raked a hand through his hair. "How could I be so stupid? Jessica knew that this was a bad idea. I should have listened."

Alex nodded. "You guys are the victims here. If it was her, we'll get her, find out how she got into your suite." Rafael sent his friend a look of thanks.

"This could work for you, Rafael," Jillian finally

spoke up. "Sex scandals hardly ever have negative blow-back on the man involved. This could be enough to drive Jessica from the race."

Rafael shook his head. "I can't do that to Jess." As the other two headed for the elevators, he hung back. "I've got to see her."

"Now?" Jillian asked him. "We've got to talk about this."

"Later," he snapped at her. Heading for the doors, he called over his shoulder, "I need to make sure she's okay."

He left the lobby and pushed again through the reporters, dodging their questions and providing them with a simple "No comment," before getting into his SUV and driving off.

Rafael arrived at Jessica's place in record time. But he hadn't gotten there first. Several reporters had set up shop on the sidewalk outside the boundaries of her property. He parked in the driveway, next to her car, and jogged to her door. He stood on her front porch, ignoring the calls of the reporters at his back for less than a minute, though it felt like an eternity, before Ben opened the door.

"Hey."

"Is Jessica home?"

"She is."

Rafael took that as a sign to enter and tried to move around Ben, who didn't budge. He stopped and rolled his eyes. "Can I come in?"

"I don't think so. She's pretty upset."

Rafael drove his fingers through his hair. "I know she is. That's why I'm here. I have to talk to her."

"You should leave."

"It's fine," he heard her say. He looked over Ben's shoulder and saw her standing just beyond the foyer. Her eyes were red-rimmed and her lips were pulled down in a frown. He knew she'd seen the tape. "He can come in."

Ben turned to her. "Are you sure? I didn't think you wanted to see anyone."

"Let him in."

Ben moved out of the way, and Rafael entered the house, immediately reaching for her. But she moved out of his grasp and walked into the living room. Rafael followed.

"Jessie, I'll be in my room, if you need me," Ben said, coming up behind her and placing his hand on her shoulder. Rafael wanted to touch her, but he didn't dare try.

When they were alone, Rafael stepped closer. He wanted to wrap his arms around her and make it all disappear. "I came by last night. You weren't here."

"I stayed in a hotel. There were too many reporters."

"Are you okay?"

Her laugh was hollow. "No. I'm not okay. I've been fielding questions from reporters all morning, and not just the ones camping outside my home. And not to mention the heat I'm taking online. People questioning my morals, my feminism, religious groups calling for my resignation from the campaign."

Rafael had had a rough morning, but it had been nothing compared to the vitriol that Jessica must have seen. "Jesus, I'm sorry, Jessica. I really don't know how this happened."

"Who leaked it?"

"I don't know."

"Was it you?"

He recoiled as if she'd slapped him. "What? That's ridiculous. Why would I do that?"

"To make me drop out of the campaign. All of this has been a ploy to get me to trust you, to love you, all so you could just get rid of me. You'd do anything to win, right?"

"No. That isn't what happened." He paused. "You love me?"

"No," she answered quickly, although he didn't quite believe her. "And let me tell you this, I'm not dropping out. I'm not a quitter. I will put up with the trolls and the abuse. I'll see it through and I will beat your ass."

"Good. I don't want you to drop out."

She ignored him and spoke over him. "And then you and your friends made that big show of getting me to perform at the club. It all makes sense now. You wanted to make sure I could be recorded. I was so stupid."

"Jess, no, I promise you. I didn't do this." He tried to meet her eyes, but she averted them. "I do want to be straight with you, though. Tanya Roberts came to see me yesterday, apparently just before the story broke. I had Gabe and the rest of the legal team on it as fast as I could. I'm sorry."

"You knew? Why didn't you tell me? A heads-up would have been nice."

"I tried. I didn't have time. And by the time she left my office it was too late. I didn't know about the video until this morning. She showed me some still photos."

"You should go." She turned away from him and he reached out and grasped her arm.

"I'm not going anywhere. You said you loved me. Whatever you were feeling for me, I was feeling it for you, *am still* feeling it for you, as well. I love you."

She said nothing. Her silence went on, making him desperate, something he hadn't felt in a long time. He didn't want to lose Jessica. He couldn't.

"Jess, believe me. I wouldn't leak it. I'm in the video, too."

"Yeah, but you're a man, it's different for you. I'm the whore that let you touch me, you're the man filling a biological need."

He grasped her forearms and forced her to look at him. "That's not how it was with us, and you know it. Certainly not that night, not any night we were together."

"This was never anything real, Rafael. You tracked me down, made me vulnerable and seduced me. Sure, it led to some pretty serious feelings, and I liked you. But how could we start a relationship like that? How could we trust each other?"

Frustrated, Rafael turned away from her. "I'm sorry about the way things started. But if you think I voluntarily seduced you as a means to an end, you're wrong.

I'm just as helpless to these feelings as you are. But I don't regret anything else when it comes to us. We had fun."

"It was fun," she said wistfully and paused. "But now you should leave."

"Jess," he said, not making any movement to leave.

She turned away from him. "Get out."

"Jess, don't do this."

"Get out!"

Rafael looked up and saw Ben standing at the banister, ready to come to Jessica's side. But Rafael didn't want any more trouble.

"Fine," he said. "I'll leave. But we aren't done." He would be back, every day, if that's what it took for her to believe him.

"We are, Rafael. It's over. Please leave me alone. I've got work to do. The election is in a couple of days. I'll see you at the polls."

CHAPTER SEVENTEEN

Rafael sat at his desk. He didn't know how things had gotten so royally fucked-up. His phone rang, and he saw that it was Alana. "Hey. How are you holding up?"

"Well I've certainly felt better," he responded, and gestured to the newspapers that were stacked on his desk. "I was caught having sex on camera with my opponent, who was outed as a stripper, on a leaked tape, and my own ties to an erotic club have also been discovered, all a few days before the election, so, I'm not doing too well."

"Come on, it's going to be okay. You aren't the only person in the public eye to have something like this get out."

He wasn't worried about himself. He'd let down a lot of people around him, and he didn't know how he would make it right again. "I saw that Di Terrestres was identified in the reports. The club doesn't need this type of press, either. How's the blowback from that?"

"Nothing yet. I just wanted to tell you that we discovered how the camera ended up in your room."

"How?"

"One of our servers came clean. He says that a contact who works for LVTV News paid him to do it. He gained access with a duplicated swipe card, and later that night, he snuck Tanya Roberts into the party."

"Motherfucker."

"Yeah, but he's fired and we're pressing charges. He broke the nondisclosure agreement, and we're combing the rest of the club to make sure there aren't any other cameras."

"Okay. I'm sorry all of this came down on the club."

"Don't be sorry. It's a storm we'll weather together. We always do. I've got to go. Let me know if you need anything."

He hung up, and when he was alone again, he glanced at the muted television, where Jessica's face appeared. He reached for the remote to hear her statement.

"...you've all seen the footage that I regret has gotten out. But I just want to tell you that I'm not ashamed. I'm not embarrassed. We live in a time when women are expected to be both sexual objects dressed and made-up to please the male gaze, but the minute we act out on our sexuality, dress how we want, behave how we want, we're called vile names. Sometimes women just can't win. There is absolutely nothing wrong with consensual sex between two adults. I just regret that I put my trust in a person and a situation that I thought was safe. I am not withdrawing from the mayoral race. I'm here until the bitter end, and I intend to win."

"What is the nature of your relationship with Councilman Martinez?" an off-camera reporter asked her.

"Councilman Martinez and I have no relationship," she answered, her voice cold and robotic. "We are competitors in the mayoral race, and we both pledge to do what we believe is best for the people of Las Vegas. Thank you."

Later that evening, Rafael stood on the front steps of the BH and addressed the press.

"Councilman Martinez, do you plan to drop out of the mayoral race, given the video of you that's come to light."

"No, of course not. What happened was a huge invasion of my privacy, and that of Councillor Morgan. There's no way I'm going to abandon my plans to be mayor. I have a job to do."

"Do you agree with the calls for Jessica Morgan to withdraw from hers?"

"Absolutely not," he said. "Ms. Morgan is an excellent candidate and a formidable opponent. It wouldn't be fair to her, me or the city for her to drop out now, this close to Election Day."

"Are you just saying that because you're romantically involved with her?"

"I'm not here to discuss my personal life. That's completely private."

"Yeah, not anymore," some nameless voice heckled from somewhere in the back.

Rafael ignored the comment, then pushed his way

inside. Alex, Brett, Gabe and Alana met him in the lobby, all frowning at the scene outside behind him. His friends closed ranks around him, blocking him from view. He was grateful for them. They protected each other.

He looked at Alex. "So, campaign manager, do you think this is a distraction from my campaign?"

"You always go big or go home, right? But it's not anything we can't handle. We're here for you."

"Thanks. Guys, I really appreciate it. I'm just upset that it could blow back on you all. Shit," he muttered. Now that the press had a taste of what went on at the club, what was to stop them from digging for more of its erotic secrets? "I'm sorry."

"Don't worry about it," Brett told him, slapping a hand on his back as they all walked to the elevator. "It isn't your fault."

"But on the upside, there has been a huge influx in people looking to join the club," Alana informed the group.

"What? Really?" Rafael asked.

She nodded. "It's true. Our concierge's office has been inundated with requests—big shots, athletes, celebrities. Your little video has put us on the map. We're working overtime to vet particular people, but it looks like our club is going to get bigger."

"Well, how about that?" Gabe said.

"And there are a lot of requests to see Jessica perform again. She was incredible."

"Yeah, I don't see that happening anytime soon."

"What did she say when you spoke to her?" Brett asked.

"She never wants to see me again."

"But now that her secret's out, people know that she performed here, at least she isn't a social pariah."

The group entered Rafael's office, and they sat around the large conference table. "Gabe, give me some good news."

"I have some. You can press charges against LVTV. If the video is online, it's pretty much there forever. Just trying to get some of those websites to take down a video where there isn't any illegal activity taking place is almost impossible."

"Just great."

"But how about you, Raf?" Alana asked. "How are you doing?"

"I've been better." He put his face in his hands, finally allowing himself to relax, to let go in front of his friends. "Everything is just so fucked-up. I embarrassed myself, Jessica, The Brotherhood, the club, my family, everything."

Alex put a hand on his shoulder. "Don't worry about us. Raf, your trust was violated just as much as Jessica's was. You didn't do anything wrong."

"She trusted me, and I didn't protect her. I could have stayed away from her. But instead, my own selfish need to see her outed us, exposed her and ruined her campaign. She thinks I was behind the video and leaking it."

"You weren't, though," Gabe needlessly reminded him. "Just go to her again. Explain it to her."

"I don't know if I can," he admitted, remembering the look on her face when she told him to leave. "The election is in a couple days. I just have to focus on getting there. No more distractions. I need to keep my head down and get to work."

"Work," Brett muttered, shaking his head.

"What's that?" Rafael asked.

"We all work too goddamn much." He addressed the group. "You all know that, right? I realized that during my honeymoon. It's nice, and normal, to unplug sometimes. Between politics and the business, and sleeping here most nights, you all spend too much of your life surrounded by it. You need to make time for the better things."

"All that work is what brings me the better things," Rafael said, looking around at the ornate office in the luxury tower they owned.

"I'm not talking about the money or success, or any of the things you can buy. I'm talking about the things that enrich the soul—love, you dumbass," he clarified. "If you love her, win her back. Because I don't think you'll ever be happy without her. I don't know where I'd be if I didn't get a second chance with Rebecca. And I almost fucked it all up with my stupid pride. Trust me. It's worth it."

"Maybe I will. After the election," Rafael agreed reluctantly. "I need to focus on the task at hand first. Winning."

"Just don't wait too long," Brett warned. "You might not be lucky enough to get a second chance."

CHAPTER EIGHTEEN

RAFAEL KNEW THE moment the mood in the room shifted. When the numbers turned against his favor, and in that of Jessica Morgan—Las Vegas's projected mayor, the youngest female mayor in the city's history, in fact. The city's women had come out in unexpected numbers to vote and there was no doubt, they loved Jessica. He huffed out a disappointed breath and raked his fingers through his hair, then looked around the room. Even though he knew hundreds of eyes were on him, none of them would make contact with his.

The writing was on the wall, and he wanted to get out of there, but he couldn't. He had to stay for his concession speech. The one he hadn't planned on making. He hadn't even written the goddamn thing.

Avoiding the eyes of those around him, Rafael crossed the room to the table where his friends stood. He stood silently with them for a moment, before Alex spoke up. "It's not looking good."

"Yeah, no shit." Rafael tried not to sound so defeated, but it was tough. Everything he'd ever achieved, he'd worked his ass off for it. Every luxury he'd been afforded was a direct result of the blood, sweat and tears that he poured into everything he undertook.

But in this endeavor, hard work hadn't been enough. He'd been beaten. In the span of a couple of days, he'd lost his dream job, and the only woman he'd ever loved.

"You know, it isn't the end of the world," Alana offered, trying to make him feel a little better.

"What about all of our plans? This was important to all of us."

Alex shook his head. "Don't worry about that. Sure, working with the mayor would have made things a little easier for us, but I don't know if you realize it, we've been pretty successful without it."

Rafael barely heard him. He looked up at the news feed that had been set up, with the local anchors announcing the numbers as they came in. But now, Jessica's face filled the screen with a ticker that called her Mayor Morgan. He looked back to his friends, and while he was grateful for their support, he missed Jessica. The past few days without her had been harder than he'd anticipated. And even though the night hadn't turned out the way he'd hoped, a part of him was still happy for her, proud of her, as he watched her image on the TV.

"Can somebody turn that off?" Brett called out to one of the party's staff members.

Rafael held up his hand. "No, don't worry about it," he said turning to the television to see her. "She won, I owe it to her to watch."

"I think it's time for your speech, man," Alex said.

Rafael nodded, and took to the podium on the stage, where he'd anticipated making his victory speech, committing himself to a term as mayor. "Hello," he started, as his guests turned their attention to him. "This isn't the speech that I'd anticipated making tonight. I'd imagined a different outcome, a more jubilant mood. But life doesn't always turn out the way you expect.

"Don't count me out yet, though. I'm not going anywhere. I may no longer be on city council, and I might not be mayor. But I still love this city, and if there's anything that Ms.—Mayor—Morgan has taught me, it's the importance of giving back. I will now strive to use my position in the business community to fight for the people of Las Vegas. And I can guarantee, you haven't heard the last from me.

"But what can I say? I ran a strong campaign, and so did Jessica Morgan. Despite everything that has happened, we both kept going. While I thought I had victory locked down, the residents of Las Vegas made their decision, they've spoken. They want her. I know that Ms. Morgan will be a phenomenal mayor, and I know that every ounce of passion she has will go into the job. She is the leader that Las Vegas deserves. So, I just want to say thank you to all my family, friends and supporters. I couldn't have even gotten here without any of you. Good night."

Without taking any questions, Rafael left the podium. He didn't have time to stick around. He had another party to get to.

* * *

Jessica found a quiet, lonely corner to catch her breath. She couldn't believe that despite every roadblock, every hurdle and the massive scandal that had followed her, she was the mayor of Las Vegas. There would be time to analyze her campaign and voter response later. She should be enjoying her moment, but her brain transitioned into *work mode*.

"Did you hear," Ben asked, finding her. "Rafael conceded."

"Already?" she asked in disbelief. The results had been close enough that no one could blame him for demanding a recount. She hadn't expected him to give up without a long, drawn-out battle.

"Congratulations, Mayor Morgan," she heard a deep, familiar voice come up behind her. She turned to see Rafael.

"What are you doing here? I expected you to be at your own party."

He shrugged. "Believe it or not, it's not very much fun to be at the losing party." He looked around. "There's a much better vibe here."

"Why are you here?"

"To congratulate you. You had a message that resonated with the community, and I realized that maybe my own reasons for running weren't so virtuous. And what can I say? The best candidate won."

"Yeah, I did," she said with a smug smile.

"I also came to see if you still hate me."

"I never hated you. I felt betrayed. Stupid, that I'd been found out. I took it out on you. It was never hate."

He looked around and noticed that people were watching them. "Can we go somewhere a little more private?"

"Yeah, come on." She led him to a smaller vestibule off the main room. She shut the door, locking out the rest of the world. She watched him, unsure of what he was doing there.

"I'm sorry," he started. "I honestly didn't know we were being recorded. And I should have listened to you when you said our affair was a risk. It was Tanya Roberts. I should have known that her being at the club was more dangerous than I'd imagined."

"I know it wasn't your fault. Alana called me." His brow furrowed. "I'm sorry I lashed out when you were betrayed and violated just as much as I was."

He nodded. "I'm sorry about everything. I'm sorry I didn't protect you better. I'm sorry I betrayed that trust and hurt you."

"Let's not talk about any of that now. It can wait." She smiled at him, suddenly feeling playful. "So, what are you going to do now? You're unemployed. Have you made any plans?"

"Rub it in," he said with a laugh. "No, I made no plans. Because I honestly thought I was going to win," he said with a shrug. "There's enough work with The Brotherhood to keep me busy before I consider a senate run. Maybe I'll take a little time off. Relax a little. See if I remember how. I was told by a friend that I work too much. I should make time for the better things. Like love."

She didn't know what else to say. She'd lashed out at him, believing the worst. Maybe it hadn't been fair. But knowing how their relationship started, she wouldn't have put it past him at the time.

"My first step to full relaxation, however, is to date more."

"Oh, really?" She frowned, not liking the thought of him seeing other women.

"Do you want to get dinner or a drink with me sometime?"

"Are you asking me out on a date?"

"Yeah. I realized that we've never been on one."

"Well, all right, then. But don't forget, it isn't going to be that easy. We have a lot of stuff to work out."

"I know we do," he agreed. "But I'm not afraid of a little hard work, are you?"

She shook her head. "I'm not, either."

Rafael stepped closer, so that her breasts brushed his chest. "I missed you," he whispered, placing his palms on the wall on either of her head, boxing her in.

"I missed you, too."

"How long before you think people start to notice you're gone?"

"I'd say we have a couple of minutes."

He chuckled. She'd missed that sound, and she closed her eyes, savoring it. "That should be long enough for now. But I'll need you to spare a couple of hours for me later this evening."

"Oh, really?"

"Yeah," he whispered in her ear, his lips grazing her lobe. "Jessica, I meant it when I said I love you. I love that you're tough, sexy, kind. You want to help people, and you don't put up with my shit, and I've never wanted someone more in my life."

"I love you, too, Raf." The words stuttered from her throat. She'd never imagined saying them, especially not to the man in front of her. She gasped when he cupped her hips and pulled them against him. She could feel that he was hard behind his zipper. And even though there was a party going on in the next room, she wanted him at that moment.

She grasped his belt and unbuckled it, then lowered his pants. She reached into his boxers and withdrew him. He groaned as he pulled his wallet from his back pocket, and she was grateful when he took out a condom. She wouldn't have been able to wait until they got home. It had to be then and there. He rolled the latex over his length and lifted her leg to wrap around his thigh, and he entered her with one push that forced the air from her lungs.

His breath was quick, and she could feel the beat of his heart as it matched her own. Jessica had had her share of sexual partners, but none of them came close to Rafael. He pulled his hips back and slammed into her again. They both made desperate noises, and Jessica reached around his shoulders, steadying herself before she fell. But she knew Rafael wouldn't let her fall. She looked in his eyes, and stayed with him as he pummeled in and out of her, feeling herself rise higher and higher, until with one push, she was thrown over the edge, and she strained and cried out, oblivious to the fact that there were people on the other side of the door. She could feel her internal muscles squeeze Rafael as he was inside of her, and he stiffened, shouting hoarsely as he came and found his release, as well.

They both caught their breaths. "Mayor Morgan," someone called from the distance. "It's time for your speech."

Jessica smiled and turned back to Rafael.

"Well, go on," he said. "Your public awaits."

Instead of walking away, Jessica put her hands on his face and pulled him to her, bringing his lips solidly against her own. She kissed him with every breath she had, reveling in the resurgence of energy that poured through her. His hands took her waist and squeezed, and he kissed her back until he pulled away.

"I love you," she whispered.

"I love you, too," he told her. "But go," he said against her lips, his voice but a whisper. "Talk to your people. This is your moment. You earned it. I'll be waiting right here when you're done."

She watched him and was still reluctant to leave. But the cheers of the crowd just out of sight caught her attention, as did their *Mor-gan* chant. And she smiled. "Don't go anywhere."

"I won't."

She headed to the next room to address her constituents. She relished the moment, but she turned her head as she took the stage and saw the man she loved in the back of the crowd, watching her as she soaked up the spotlight. She knew he wasn't going anywhere.

Jessica took her place behind the podium. "Ladies and gentlemen," she started. "You can't imagine how amazing and unbelievable it is to be standing in front of you all tonight as the new mayor of Las Vegas."

The crowd cheered. "But it wasn't a solo journey. Many people helped support me on this crazy ride. Thank you for taking a chance on me. Despite everything that has happened, I haven't lost the support of the people in this city. And know that I will be here to fight for you. To all of you who came out in record numbers to vote, you will not be forgotten. Thank you all. This means so much to me. Thank you!"

She left the stage, and found Rafael again. "Let's get out of here. I'm starving."

Rafael looked around. "I'm sure there's a guy with a tray of cocktail shrimp around here somewhere."

"No. There's a twenty-four-hour diner not far from here. Don't think I've forgotten that night in San Francisco. You still owe me a late-night breakfast, remember?"

He smiled. She was looking for a fresh start. A redo on their relationship. He extended his arm and she took it. "Well, Mayor Morgan, don't think that because you won the election, I'll blindly follow your every command."

With a laugh, she said, "I never thought that for a second. Let's go."

* * * * *

COMING SOON!

We really hope you enjoyed reading this book. If you're looking for more romance, be sure to head to the shops when new books are available on

Thursday
4th October

MILLS & BOON

LET'S TALK
Romance

For exclusive extracts, competitions
and special offers, find us online:

facebook.com/millsandboon

@millsandboonuk

@millsandboon

Or get in touch on 0844 844 1351*

For all the latest titles coming soon, visit
millsandboon.co.uk/nextmonth